GONE

GONE – BOOK ONE

Stacy Claflin

Print Edition

http://www.stacyclaflin.com

Edited by Garrett Robinson

This is a work of fiction. Any resemblance to actual persons living or dead, businesses, events, or locales is purely coincidental or used fictitiously. The author has taken great liberties with locales including the creation of fictional towns.

To receive book updates from the author, sign up here.
http://bit.ly/10NrfMw

Watching

SITTING IN HIS warm truck across from the park, Chester Woodran watched her walk across the open field. An overhead light turned on as she passed under it in the dusk. Her long, dark hair swished back and forth behind her. She wandered around the playground, walking between the climbers and slides until she stopped in front of the swings.

He had spent hours watching her. Studying her. He knew her almost better than she knew herself.

The moment of truth would arrive soon. She'd come a few minutes early, but he wouldn't deviate from the schedule. He would act exactly on time. He'd laid the groundwork. He wasn't going to let her change a thing.

Chester pulled out his phone and scrolled through the pictures, stopping at his favorite. It was the girl in the park for sure, although he couldn't see the details of her face up close yet. He would have to wait a few minutes.

From the phone, her light brown eyes shone at him. Her shy, almost insecure face smiled sweetly.

His heart sped up at the thought of many weeks of work coming together at long last. The waiting was about to end.

Clenching the steering wheel with all his might, he took several deep breaths to calm himself. Every precaution had been taken. Prepared with painstaking care. There was no chance of anything going wrong so long as he stayed with the plan.

The alarm on his digital wristwatch beeped. He turned it off and then leaned back into the seat, adjusting his over-sized glasses.

It was time.

Taken

MACY MERCER SAT on the swing, clutching the cold, metal chain. Soon she'd meet Jared, the sweet and adorable boy she met online. She pushed the dirt with her foot, swinging back and forth, listening to the leaves rustle nearby as a breeze picked up. The temperature felt like it had dropped ten degrees, so she zipped up her hoodie as far as it would go. She should have worn a coat, but it was too late to go back home.

A crow cawed in the distance, giving her the chills.

To distract herself, she grabbed the new smart phone she'd received for her fifteenth birthday. She checked the time. Jared still had another five minutes. Macy had been so eager to meet him that she'd sneaked out of her house a little early, eager for her first real date. Her parents had a stupid, outdated rule that she couldn't date until she turned sixteen. There was no way she would wait an entire year. Not when her friends all went out every weekend.

She looked around the empty park once more, the swing chains groaning as they carried her back and forth listlessly. Jared was supposed to meet her after his baseball practice. He was the star of the team, and sometimes had to stay a little late because the coach expected more from him than anyone else. She scrolled through their latest texting conversation, her excitement building.

The phone buzzed, startling her. Hoping that it was Jared, she scrolled to the bottom of the screen and smiled.

Sorry, coach is keeping me late

Macy sighed, shivering in the cold Washington breeze. *How long?*

Abt a half hr

The last thing Macy wanted was to put the date off, but it was really cold. *U sure 2day still works?*

You want my dad to get u?

Macy ran her hands through her freshly-styled hair. Going with a grown man hadn't been part of the plan. She was just supposed to meet Jared and go the mall, or maybe a movie or to the arcade. They were going to play it by ear.

Is it ok? Or u wanna wait?

It was getting colder, and no way she wanted to sit here that long. The mall was too far to walk to, but with his dad she'd be warmer and see Jared sooner.

They'd talked for so long over computers and texts. Macy didn't want to wait more. She'd show everyone she wasn't afraid to go out with a boy, no matter what her parents said.

She texted him back. *He's ok driving me*?

He offered

U can't come now?

No. I have to help

Ok. Your dad can pick me up

K c u soon

Sliding the phone back into her pocket, she looked around again. Something didn't feel right, but she pushed it aside. She and Jared had known each other for a whole month, and he was sweet and funny. If he thought it was okay for her to go with his dad, it was fine. She wasn't a little girl anymore. Macy held her chin a little higher.

A green pickup truck with a black canopy pulled into the empty parking lot. Macy squinted, trying to see if the driver looked like an old version Jared's profile pictures. She couldn't tell.

The lights flashed the high beams, and she took that as her cue to go. She held her handbag close, stood tall, and walked to the truck trying to look mature and sophisticated.

As she neared the truck, the passenger door opened. The man sitting in the driver's seat looked nice enough. He had dark, straight hair with a receding hairline and big, geeky glasses. He kind of reminded her of her biology teacher, who always cracked science jokes that only he laughed at.

"Macy?" He readjusted his glasses and ran his hands through his hair.

"Yeah." She leaned all of her weight on her left foot, biting the right side of her lower lip.

He gave her an awkward smile. "I'm Jared's dad. He said you needed a ride to his practice?"

She nodded. The car radio played classic rock, like what her dad listened to. She relaxed a little.

He patted the bench seat. "Come on in. He's almost done with practice."

"Okay." Macy climbed in and closed the door. The warm air felt good after being out in the cold. She buckled in. "Thanks for the ride."

"No problem. Jared didn't want you sitting outside in the cold. Did you have a good day?"

"Sure." She shrugged. "Just school and stuff."

He pulled out of the parking lot and turned right. His phone made robot noises, and he pulled it up to his ear. "Jared. What's going on?...Yeah, she's here with me...Oh, okay. I'll let her know." He put the phone away. "Jared has to stay a little longer. Hey, I have a quick errand. Mind if I run to the hardware store before dropping you off at his school?"

"Well, how much longer is he going to be?" Macy spun a ring around her finger, nervous. "Maybe I should go back home. I can always meet him a different day. It's okay."

"I get it. I'll take you to the school. I don't want you to feel uncomfortable. You don't even know me."

"Or back to the park. I can just walk back home." Her heart pounded. Something wasn't right.

"Jared will be so disappointed. Let me take you to the school. I didn't mean to creep you out." He turned and smiled at her. "I wasn't thinking."

She sighed. "Okay." At least she would be able to get out of the truck. She could take a bus back home, or if worse came to worse she could always call her parents. She'd be grounded for sneaking out, but that might not be so bad. Just so long as she could get out of the truck.

Macy's stomach twisted in a knot, growing tighter the farther they went. Her mouth grew increasingly dry. She watched as street sign after street sign passed by.

"Maybe I should go back. I think I might have forgotten something at home."

"Oh? Are you sure?"

"Yeah. I need to go back home."

"Well, if you really think so. I'll break the news to Jared. I'm sure he'll understand." He pulled out his phone and activated the voice command. "Call Jared."

"Wait."

"Yes?"

"Well, uh...." Since he was being so nice, maybe she was overreacting. "You don't have to call him."

"If you're sure." He pushed a button on his phone and put it back in his pocket.

Macy took a deep breath. She needed to pull herself together or he might think she was immature. What if he didn't want Jared to see her? She sat taller and flipped her hair back.

He turned left down a road where he should have gone right.

"Wait," Macy said. "Jared's school is the other way."

"I know."

Her blood ran cold. "What...do you mean?"

The door locked beside her. "We're not going to a school."

"Where are we going?" She clutched her purse tightly against her.

"We're going for a drive, Macy."

"I don't want to. Take me home."

"You're not going back home."

Her heart beat so loud, it sounded like it was in her ears. She pulled on the door handle, but it wouldn't budge.

"Child locks. You can't open it from the inside."

She felt light-headed. "What about Jared?"

"There is no Jared, sweetie."

Her breath caught. "Did you kill him?"

He laughed. "That's hilarious. No, *I'm* Jared."

The blood drained from her face. "You...mean...?"

"I'm the one you've been talking to all this time."

Macy's stomach turned. She was sure she would throw up. "You're lying."

"No. It was me that you shared all your secrets with. All I had to do was throw on a picture of some random kid I found online. Everything else was me."

"You better take me back home. Once my parents figure out I'm missing, they can have the cops go through my laptop. They'll be able to track your IP address. I know that much."

"That's the thing. Before I picked you up, I was in your room and I reset your computer to factory settings. No one is going to find a thing."

Macy's head swam. "No you didn't. My parents are home. You're totally lying. Just let me go, and I swear I won't ever tell anyone about this."

He turned the music down. "I got in using your code to the garage right after you left. You mom was reading her Kindle in your parents' bedroom, like you told me she always does. Your dad was in his office on his computer. They didn't hear a thing. I went into your room and took care of your computer."

"Liar. You'd have to know my password."

"Ducky256."

She gasped. "How did you know that? I never told you."

"You didn't have to. You told me enough. Ducky is the pet ferret you got not too long ago. After your cat died, right? Snowflake, right? And 256 is your student number at school. You gave me everything I needed without even knowing it. From there, it was easy to figure out your various passwords. I had to ask innocent enough questions, and it all came together." He looked at her again, raising his bushy eyebrows.

"I don't believe you went into my house. You're just saying that."

He tossed a small, framed picture at her. She picked it up and stared at it. It was a picture of her family. She had looked at that very picture before she sneaked out. He *had* been there. Had he seen her looking at it?

"But, why? Why me?" And then, the question too terrifying to ask: what did he plan to do with her?

"That's a long story. I'm going to save that for later. Now really isn't the time."

Macy took several deep breaths, trying to calm herself down. If she was going to get away, she had to think clearly. She knew that much.

Maybe he was lying about the child locks. She would try to unlock it again when they stopped. If it opened, she would run before he knew what had happened.

"Can you tell me something? You must have a good reason. I mean, really. You spent hours and hours chatting and texting with me. Did you choose me for a reason, or was I the only girl who would talk to you?"

"It was you. I actually tried a few different personas until I found one you paid any attention to. For whatever reason, you liked Jared."

"But why? What's so special about me?" Macy asked.

"You look exactly like her. It took me a long time to find you. I spent weeks online looking for someone close to her age who looks exactly like her. I almost gave up, thinking it was impossible, but then I found your profile picture. I actually couldn't believe it. You look so much like her, you could be her."

"Her? Who her?"

"My Heather."

"What happened to Heather? Where is she?"

"You ask too many questions. You need to stop."

"But you—"

"See this?" He held up a flashlight as long as his arm.

"Yeah. Why?"

"I told you no more questions." He swung it and hit Macy on the side of her head.

Everything went black.

Gone

Alyssa Mercer finished putting on the final touches of mascara, and then stood back to look at herself before nodding in approval. She looked good, and she knew it. She was going to make everyone at the gym jealous again. No one ever thought she could be the mom of two teenagers, and that's the way she liked it. When she was out with them, she was often taken for their sister.

She picked up her curling iron and perfected a couple of curls before returning to the bedroom. Her eyes fell on the clock. She'd still have time to stop for a skinny latte before working out. Pulling her workout shoes from under her bed, she slipped them on and went into the hall.

The house was quiet. The kids were probably still sleeping. They would sleep into the afternoon if she or her husband didn't wake them. As she passed Macy's room, she could smell the ferret cage. Why had she let Macy talk her into getting the thing? It was cute, but if they didn't keep the cage clean it got smelly fast. Alyssa was going to have to tell her—again—that they would get rid of Ducky if Macy didn't keep it up.

Going down the stairs, she tripped over a pair of pants and grumbled under her breath. She had followed the books since they were little, teaching them the value of chores as toddlers. It never stuck. As they got older, it even seemed to backfire. Alyssa picked up the pants and threw them to the top of the stairs.

She readjusted her black and purple velour pants and went to the kitchen. Smoothie bags filled the fridge, and Alyssa emptied one into the blender, with some fat-free milk and fresh bananas. As it blended, she went over everything she needed to do that day.

When it was ready she poured it into a glass, leaned against the counter, and drank her breakfast. She set the empty glass in the sink, turned around, and nearly bumped into her thirteen-year-old.

"Alex, what are you doing?"

He looked disoriented. Probably because he was awake before noon. His brown, wavy hair stuck out in twenty directions and for some reason, he looked pale. Alex looked up at her, and looking into his eyes Alyssa knew something was wrong.

"What's going on?"

He blinked a few times. "Have you seen Macy's wall?"

"No. Why? Did I miss a personality quiz?" The joke sounded weak, even to her.

He pulled his tablet from his bathrobe pocket and held the screen up to her face. She took it from him and looked at his news feed, not seeing anything important. "Tell Charlie he needs to watch his language."

Alex took the tablet and looked at it. He looked like he was going to be sick. "No, Mom, it got pushed down." He scrolled down and pointed to his sister's latest status update.

Alyssa's heart sped up as she read it. "Is that some kind of joke?"

"She's not in her room." He stared at her so intently, it felt like he was looking right through her.

Without a word, Alyssa ran past Alex and back upstairs, bursting through Macy's door. It looked like her daughter was in bed. She ran to the bed and pulled away the blankets. Several large stuffed animals lay strategically to look like Macy was there. How long had she been gone?

Her heart and mind were both racing. She looked around the room for any clues. Macy's laptop was on her desk. Alyssa sat down, feeling light-headed. She opened the laptop and turned it on.

It didn't start up like it should. It took too long. Then it prompted her to set up the computer. Had Macy erased everything? She couldn't have. She wasn't technologically inclined. She was always asking Alyssa for help with it.

"It's true?"

Alyssa turned around to see Alex standing in the doorway, looking ill. "She couldn't have gone far," Alyssa said. "She's probably just mad because we won't let her date."

She cursed her husband under her breath. She and Chad had argued over that point countless times. Alyssa had never even convinced him to let Macy go on group dates. He didn't want boys anywhere near her. She had told him that Macy would rebel.

She had told him. Alyssa buried her face into her hands, feeling dizzy.

"I'm going to get Dad."

Alyssa nodded, not even looking up. She had to do something. She pulled her cell phone from her pocket and called Macy's number. She would tell Macy that the age restriction was lifted. Who cared what Chad wanted? She had to get her baby back.

The call went straight to voice mail. She listened to the entire message, feeling a small sense of relief at hearing her daughter's voice. She ended the call, doubtful that Macy would get the message if she had turned her phone off. Alyssa found Zoey's number and called. Zoey was Macy's best friend. She would know what was going on.

"Hello?" Zoey sounded half-asleep.

"Zoey, this is Macy's Mom."

"Mrs. Mercer? What's up?"

"Have you talked with Macy?"

"Uh…no. Why?"

Alyssa took a deep breath. "Did she say anything to you about running away?"

"What? No. Oh, crap. This is bad."

"Yes, this is very bad. Anything you know will help. Don't worry about getting her into trouble. We need to find her. That's the only thing that matters."

"I'm guessing you didn't know about her date last night."

"Her what?"

Zoey sighed. "She was getting together with a guy she met online."

The room shrank around Alyssa. "What…?"

"Yeah. Jared something. Wait. Hold on. He messaged me on online, asking some questions about her. Let me look."

Alyssa took several deep breaths as she listened to the rustling sounds of Zoey on the other end of the line. Things were going from bad to worse.

"I can't find his message, Mrs. Mercer. Wait a minute. Oh, I see the problem. He deactivated his account. I can still see the messages, but his name's gone, and there's no picture. I wish I could remember his last name. Is Macy going to be okay?"

"I hope so. Listen, Zoey, if you hear anything else, or think of anything, call me back. Okay?"

"Yeah, sure. I'll see if I can find anything else."

"Thanks. Bye."

"Bye, Mrs. Mercer. I'll do anything to help find her."

Alyssa nodded, knowing, and not caring, that Zoey couldn't see her. She opened the app on her phone and went to her daughter's profile, searching for clues.

Awake

THE GROUND BENEATH Macy bumped up and down, waking her. She looked around, her head pounding, and reached for the side of her head. A tender bump stuck out near her forehead. The last thing she remembered was going into the truck with the madman who had pretended to be Jared.

She rolled to the side of the truck, slamming her already-sore head as they took a sharp turn. On all fours, she crawled to the back of the truck to see if she could unlock it. Everything was sealed tight. Not that she was surprised, given how much effort the guy had gone to with everything else.

The two of them had spent hours and hours messaging and texting. "Jared" had always seemed so interested in her, like she was special. But all he really wanted was to figure out her passwords. She wanted to kick herself; her parents had told her countless times not to give out personal information online. She had thought Jared was safe, but she had obviously been wrong.

Macy went to the sides of the truck, feeling around for anything she could open. She searched every single inch of the truck bed and canopy. It was no use; he had made sure everything was locked. All she found was a blanket, folded up and tucked into a corner.

Where was he taking her? And who was Heather? That name seemed important to him. Maybe if Macy could figure out why, she could figure out a way to escape.

The truck stopped, and the engine cut. Her stomach rumbled, and Macy realized how hungry she was. She hadn't eaten anything since lunch, and who knew how long ago that had been? She'd been planning to eat with Jared, who didn't even exist. She leaned against the corner of the walls.

Minutes ticked by as she waited. She shivered and grabbed the blanket, wrapping it around herself. It had the light scent of a girl's perfume.

As she started to doze, a loud click snapped her back to reality. The door of the canopy opened and the madman looked in. "Good. You're awake. I got some food. You'd better eat it because we're not stopping again for a while." He threw a wrapped hamburger at her. "I know you're vegan, but that's what you're getting. Eat it or go hungry."

He lowered the canopy door.

"Wait! Where are we going?"

"You'll find out soon enough." The door slammed, and Macy heard the lock slide into place.

She stared at the hamburger, sitting on the blanket. She hadn't eaten meat in more than six months, but her stomach roared, begging her to eat the greasy, dead animal.

The irony didn't escape her. Macy had gone vegan to lose weight, tired of everyone calling her "Muffin-top Macy." She'd lost the weight, but the name had stuck. That's what had led her to seek a boyfriend online. Now, here she was.

She wouldn't let the psycho win. She wasn't going to eat his burger. He might have poisoned it, anyway, or slipped something in to make her more agreeable.

She'd show him. If he saw she couldn't be controlled that easily, maybe he would give up and let her go. She had skipped meals plenty of times. When she first went vegan, her parents hadn't taken her seriously and continued to serve meat-filled meals.

Once they figured out that she would starve herself if that's what it took, they changed their minds—and Macy's diet.

She threw the burger across the truck. She wasn't going to eat it. If nothing else, it would take off a little more weight.

She leaned her head against the wall of the truck bed, tired and scared. There was no getting away yet, she knew that. So she let herself fall asleep again, thinking that at least she might be rested when the time came to escape.

The truck went over a large bump, waking her. How long had she been asleep this time? She could smell the cold hamburger. It permeated the entire truck bed. Her stomach rumbled again, but it twisted at the same time. As hungry as she was, the burger was the last thing she wanted to eat.

Pulling the perfumed blanket up close to her chin, she wanted to go back to sleep. No, what she wanted was to go back in time and never talk to "Jared" in the first place. Why had she been so stupid? Why hadn't she changed her passwords more often? She'd always heard how important that was.

Before long, boredom struck. It felt strange to be bored when she could be killed any moment, but the waiting was the worst part. Waiting wasn't her strong suit—but really, was it anyone's?

Of course, she knew that once the truck stopped she would probably give anything to be bored again.

How was she going to fight him? She should know something about self-defense given how many hours she'd been forced to watch her brother's karate tournaments and practices. There was something to do with pressure points, but she couldn't remember what. She had never paid any attention, usually playing a game, texting, or reading.

Why hadn't she agreed to take the lessons with him? The sound of her dad's voice telling her that it would be good for her bounced around her head. Why hadn't she listened? There were so many things Macy would have done differently, if only she'd known. So many things.

The truck hit another bump, and as Macy went into the air she realized she had to go to the bathroom. Bad. What was she supposed to do? Peeing in his truck would have made her happy, but she didn't want to have to smell it, or worse, land in it at some point.

They went over another bump, and she knew that she had to do something before she lost control of her bladder. The last thing she wanted was to soak her clothes. Macy squeezed her pelvic muscles and looked around in desperation. She noticed something behind one of the tires. Was that some kind of container? Why hadn't she noticed that before? Her stomach sank as she realized it was there for her to pee in.

Holding her breath to keep control of her bladder, she crawled over to it. It was an empty juice jug. That was going to have to do the job. They hit another bump, and she dropped the container as she leaked a few drops of urine. "Crap!" She scrambled for the jug and, feeling like an idiot, dropped her pants.

When she was done, a feeling of relief washing over her entire body, Macy grabbed the lid and twisted as tight as she could get it. If she knew she was getting out soon, she would relieve herself in a corner to spite him.

She pulled her pants back up and returned to the blanket. It was so cold, and she was starting to shiver. Lowering her pants hadn't helped. Even with the blanket, she hadn't been warm enough. As she settled down with the blanket, the pee jug caught her eye.

Oh, that was gross. How could she even think that?

But it *was* warm, she couldn't deny that.

No. She would wait. She wasn't going to warm up with a pitcher of her pee. Macy looked at the ceiling, but before long, she was shivering.

Shoving the blanket aside, she crawled over to the container and brought it back to the blanket. Sticking it in her lap, she pulled the blanket over her again. The warmth from the pee felt good, as disgusting as that was. Macy imagined it was one of those heat packets she put in her pockets when they went skiing.

Macy must have fallen asleep again, because the jerk of the truck stopping woke her up. She blinked her eyes, trying to get her bearings. She felt groggy, and that had to mean she had been asleep for a while. Were they out of state? When she had been in the cab of the truck, they were heading east, more than likely leaving Washington. But where?

The canopy opened again. Her abductor looked around, and then smiled when he saw her.

"Don't get any funny ideas. If you try to escape, I'll go back and kill your entire family."

"What?"

"I got in once. I can do it again. If you get away, I'll go after them instead of you. Well, I will go after you too, don't get me wrong." He laughed. What a freaking psycho.

Macy shuddered.

"You still haven't eaten the burger I was nice enough to get you? Get one thing straight: you're not getting anything else to eat until you finish that first."

"But it's old and gross."

"Maybe you should have thought of that when I gave it to you. Don't test me, girl. I will wait as long as it takes for you to eat it before I give you anything else. It saves me money."

"But you know I don't eat meat."

"Looks like you're going to have to. It's going to be even less enjoyable as cold as it is. I wouldn't let it get any older, because it's sure not going to get better."

"Where are you taking me?"

"You'll find out soon enough. Eat the burger."

"What'll you do if I don't?"

"Don't you listen? I won't give you anything else to eat. I need some rest, so we're going to stop for a bit. Eat that damn burger, if you know what's good for you."

He slammed the canopy door shut, and locked it. Tears filled Macy's eyes. Was he serious about killing her family? He was crazy enough to kidnap her, so he was probably serious about killing them.

They hadn't done anything wrong. This whole situation was on Macy, and she knew it. She had been the one stupid enough to get herself into the truck in the first place. She would have to figure something out.

Her stomach rumbled again. Macy looked at the burger, disgusted. Would he really make her eat it? Why did he care what she ate? There had to be a way she could hide it, so he would think she ate it. Where? There weren't exactly hiding places in the truck bed.

She tried to focus on calming her stomach. Once it relaxed, she stared at the burger, imagining she was having a staring contest with it.

"I'm losing my mind," she muttered. If she was going to eat it, it needed to be soon. The burger wouldn't get any fresher. Which was the more appealing choice? To starve, or to eat the cold, greasy burger? She would have chosen to go hungry, except that she didn't want to be forced to eat it a day or two later. At least it was somewhat edible right now.

The minutes ticked by as Macy stared at the burger. But the more she thought about it, the more she thought about having to eat it days down the road. That convinced her. She crawled across the cab and carried the burger back to the blanket.

"I'm sorry," she said to the cow she was about to eat. She unwrapped the waxy paper, and looked at the wilted bun, shaking her head. Her stomach growled, begging her to give it the nourishment.

Closing her eyes, she bit down. The cold grease shocked her taste buds, and she had to force herself not to spit it out. The way it felt as she chewed it up only made it worse. It stank too. She plugged her nose, and took another bite, relieved to discover she almost couldn't taste it.

She shoveled it in, eating as fast as she could without choking. Macy tried to pretend she was eating a veggie burger, but it didn't work. It was an old, disgusting slab of meat cooked in grease, no matter what she told herself.

After finally finishing it, she threw the wrapper and tried to ignore how disgusting she felt. Her skin felt oily from the grease, and her stomach didn't feel right. Hopefully once it settled she would have more energy for getting away—if she could.

Interrupted

CHAD MERCER WAS typing at his typical 120 words per minute when there was a knock on the door. He ignored it. His family knew to leave him alone when the door was closed.

The knocking continued, distracting him. Why couldn't they let him get his work done? Well, it wasn't actually work. Not yet, anyway. He had a popular sports blog, where he posted his opinions. People loved his sense of humor, and he always had good statistics.

With his monthly page views and low bounce rate, he was able to get a lot of really good advertising on his site that actually paid some of the bills.

He was popular online. People loved him. Unlike at home, where no one appreciated him.

The knocking wouldn't stop, and Chad lost the funny quip he'd been searching for. He sighed. "What is it?"

"Dad! Let me in!" Alex pounded on the door again.

Chad shook his head. "You know I'm busy." When would they ever start appreciating what he was trying to do for the family? His wife already didn't have to work, but no one seemed to care.

"Dad! Macy's gone!"

Gone? He got up and unlocked the door, and then opened it. "What do you mean, she's gone?"

"She's not here. She posted something online about running away."

Shaking his head, Chad went back to his desk. He minimized his blog and opened up a new window. Nothing from Macy showed up on his news feed. He typed in her name to pull up her profile. Sure enough, her latest update was one big, public tongue-sticking at him.

The house phone rang next to him. He looked over, seeing the caller ID. It was his in-laws. His mother-in-law must have stopped playing Sugar Saga for three minutes and seen Macy's update. He shook his head. Alyssa was going to chew him out. They had argued nonstop about Macy and what age she should be allowed to date.

Alyssa had told him countless times that he needed to give Macy room to grow up or she would rebel. Macy had been giving him attitude for a while, and now she had taken it public. This was just a publicity stunt. His daughter wanted to rally support.

Chad's cell phone rang. He picked it up from his desk. It was Valerie Carter, Zoey's mom. He clicked ignore and put it back down.

"What are you going to do?"

He had forgotten Alex was still there. His son looked like he was going to be sick. Macy would never believe how worried her brother was about her. With all his teasing and picking on her, he still adored his sister.

Chad took a deep breath. "I'm going to look online and see where her phone is. You guys have those Child Protect phones where the GPS tracking can't be turned off." He turned to his computer screen, went to the site that tracked the kids' phones and logged in. He could only see Alex's phone, which of course was at their address.

He scrolled the site for contact information and called them. When someone answered, he interrupted them before they could say two words.

"I have one of your Child Protect phones, and my daughter's phone isn't showing up. Mind telling me what's going on? I was told that this couldn't happen."

"Sir, if the battery has been removed, we can't track the GPS. It has to have the battery."

"What good are you? Do you know how much we pay for these? I want a refund!"

"If you calm down and give me your information, we can—"

"My kid is missing. You guys are supposed to be a technology company. Use it to figure out who I am and then send me a refund check." He ended the call. "Dipsticks."

The house phone rang again. This time it was Sandra McMillan from the homeowners' association.

When he found Macy, he was going to give her the punishment of a lifetime.

"How are we going to find Macy?"

Chad looked back up at Alex. His lips trembled.

Did Macy think of no one besides herself? First with the whole vegetarian—no, "vegan" thing, and now this. Did she find joy in making him miserable? He could see her sitting somewhere, laughing at the stress she was putting everyone through. All because he wouldn't let her to go on a date. After this stunt, she wouldn't be going on any dates until she graduated.

The home phone rang again, and this time he took the batteries out. That girl had close to a thousand friends on social media, and now every single one of them knew she had run away. Chad took a deep breath and then turned to his son again. "Do you know anything else? Anything besides what's in her update?"

Alex shook his head.

"Well, I guess she'll come home when she's hungry. Why don't you go check on your mother?"

Alex nodded, and Chad was struck by how much his usually tough son looked like a little boy. It was easy to forget how young thirteen really was. The look on his face reminded Chad of when Alex was a preschooler, chasing after his big sister and wanting to do everything she did.

For a moment Chad thought he should give his son a hug, but he stiffened. There was no need for that. "Don't worry about her. She's trying to scare us. I'll bet you she's at Zoey's house hiding out. She's going to lose her phone for a long time for this one. Don't you ever try it."

Alex didn't look convinced. He turned around and left the room.

Chad ran his hands through his hair. If only his parents were still alive. There was nothing better than talking with his dad when he had a problem. He had always had a level head and could point Chad in the right direction. They had been killed in a car accident when the kids were really young, so he hadn't had their advice for any of his parenting questions.

Sick

MACY'S HEAD SLAMMED into the truck's side and she woke up, realizing she'd fallen asleep again. She rubbed the new bump, hoping they would stop soon. Her stomach felt worse than it had after eating the burger. The movement of the truck hadn't helped, she was sure. The motion and the bumps wreaked havoc on her.

Her stomach lurched, and she turned her head in time to throw up without getting anything on the blanket.

She wiped her mouth and put her forehead against her knees, crying so hard she shook. What had she done to deserve this?

What if it got worse? What did that psycho have in store for her? Would he really kill her family? Or was that something kidnappers said to keep their victims in line?

Some kid in the news had recently escaped after being grabbed at the mall. Hadn't Macy heard that that kidnapper had made the same threats? He never killed the kid's family. But he was also in jail.

Macy closed her eyes, still breathing through her mouth to avoid the smell of her own puke. She figured she might try to get more sleep, because who knew what would happen once they stopped? All she knew was she would need to think and act fast.

As she drifted off, she breathed in through her nose. Immediately she gagged at the smell of her own vomit. Being trapped in the enclosed bed of the truck made the stench even more unbearable.

The truck slowed to a stop. She could hear the engine cut and the driver's side door slam shut. Footsteps on gravel came closer. Macy's heart pounded, and when she heard the key turning close, her heart nearly leapt out of her throat.

She breathed in fresh air as the back opened up. Macy covered her eyes in the bright sun. When her eyes adjusted, her eyes focused on her captor.

His mouth formed into a cruel twist. "What is that smell?"

"My stomach couldn't handle your burger."

"You're going to have to clean that up, you know." His bushy eyebrows came together.

Macy scooted back. "With what? It's not even my fault."

"Shut up. I was kind enough to get you food and even a blanket, and this is how you repay me? Close your trap and clean my truck. That's disgusting." His scary glare bore into Macy's eyes.

"You were kind enough—?"

"I said shut up!" He put his face less than an inch from Macy's. "Find a way to clean it up. You made the mess, you clean it. Got it?"

Macy blinked, but she kept quiet.

"Got it?" he yelled. His coffee-scented spit splattered on her face. The smell made her stomach turn again.

She wiped her face. "Don't yell at me."

"I'll yell at you if I want to. You destroyed my property. The acid in that will eat my paint. Get it cleaned up! Do you understand?"

"Okay."

"Good." The door slammed and locked again.

Her lips shook, and her eyes filled with tears. He had done this to her, and now he expected her to clean the mess? With what? Did he actually think he had done anything kind to her? He was a monster.

The hot tears spilled onto her face. She wiped them with her sleeve. Her nose dripped, so she wiped that too.

The smell of the vomit made its way back to her nose. Her stomach lurched again, but she was determined to keep it down this time. She had to have some kind of control over something.

The door unlocked, opened slightly, and something soft bounced toward her. Then something hard and loud landed a few feet away. The door slammed and locked again. Wiping her tears away, she picked up the object next to her. It was a roll of paper towels. She reached for the other thing. It was some kind of spray bottle.

"Get cleaning!" the guy shouted from the outside of the truck.

Her adrenaline pumped. Macy wanted to choke him the next time he opened the door. Wrap her hands around his neck and squeeze as hard as she could. Her hands clenched, breaking the skin.

Macy pulled off a paper towel and wiped her face, then blew her nose. She threw the towels in a corner, held her breath, and grabbed the spray bottle.

Crawling to the mess, she began to whisper, "I hate you. I hate you. I hate you." She ripped off several paper towels and wiped at the mess. She had to breathe through her mouth, and with every breath in and out she kept cursing him under her breath. She threw the towels to the side and grabbed more, soaking up the mess until it was gone. Then she grabbed the spray bottle.

Whatever was in there reeked of chemicals. It made her nose burn and gave her a headache. She wiped the floor where she had sprayed, hoping the headache wouldn't last. When she thought she had the whole mess cleaned up—it was hard to tell with such little light—she threw the paper towels with the others and went back to the blanket.

She sat in the corner and wiped away sweat. The air was cold and soon she was shivering, even with a hoodie. She played with a nail as she waited. He was taking forever and the chemical smell was making her head spin.

After a while, the driver's side door slammed again, and the engine started. Her head throbbed. How much further did they have to go?

Macy had seen enough TV to know this could get ugly.

Rubbing her temples, she tried to push those thoughts out of her mind. But as soon as she pushed one away, another would replace it.

She knew enough to know that by forcing her to eat the meat, he was trying to show her he was in control. She also knew that anyone who needed to control others was actually scared and weak, despite their actions.

She'd heard a quote somewhere, probably at school, that said something along the lines of abusers and bullies being scared little boys and girls deep down. People who were happy and confident didn't treat people bad. Maybe Macy could find his weakness and use it to her advantage.

Head pounding, she leaned against the wall again. The road had grown bumpier, and somehow it helped to lull her to sleep despite the jostling. She didn't wake up until the truck stopped.

Her head still hurt as she came awake, but it wasn't as bad as it had been. Before she knew it the lock turned again, and both the door to the canopy and the truck bed opened.

Bright light shone in Macy's eyes, and she had to cover them with her arm. Her headache made the rays of light slice like razor blades.

The man grabbed her shirt, and yanked her out of the truck. Outside the light was even worse, but at least she could breathe easier. Her head even felt a little relief until he slammed her against the side of the truck with both hands.

He stared her down, less than an inch away from her face, and he narrowed his eyes. She had never seen anyone so angry before. He tightened his grip on her shoulders and pushed her against the truck again. "Don't you ever—*ever*—talk back to me again. Do you understand? When I tell you to do something, you do it! Don't question me." He dug his fingers into her shoulder, and she could feel her skin bruise. "Do you understand?" he shouted.

She nodded, afraid to speak.

"Good. Now come with me." He grabbed her arm and yanked so hard that she thought he might have pulled it out of the socket.

Macy walked behind him, trying to keep up. He never stopped squeezing; she could feel his fingers squeezing down to the bone. She looked around, trying to figure out where they were. To their left, she saw fields of corn close by. Straight ahead, she could see a farmhouse and a dilapidated red barn. They appeared to be heading for the barn.

"What are we doing?"

"I told you not to talk back!" He stopped, turned and stared her down, squeezing her arm even harder. "Don't speak unless spoken to. Ever again."

She looked away, and he yanked her along again. Macy couldn't help rolling her eyes. *Ever again*? Seriously? For a scared little boy, he was sure full of himself. She had to hold onto the image of him as a frightened child if she was going to keep her sanity. She wouldn't let herself develop

Stockholm syndrome and feel sorry for the creep. She was going to get away. She was.

They went through the barn door and Macy looked around, trying to figure out what he had in mind. She half-expected to see the barn converted into a torture chamber, but it was just a barn. A couple of horses stood to the left, some cows off to the right, and she could hear sheep somewhere. The smell of manure was all around, but after being trapped with the smell of her own vomit, it was a welcome scent.

Rays of light shone through some of the rafters above, and dust danced through them. The fact that the sun could get through the walls encouraged her. She probably could too if she tried hard enough. They walked through the length of the barn, and stopped near some empty stalls.

He bent over, forcing her to join him as he clutched her arm. He brushed aside some hay from the floor and lifted up a round piece of metal. A trap door opened up.

Macy held her breath. She'd been wrong. He'd built the torture chamber beneath the barn, not inside it.

Frantic

ALYSSA STOOD FROM Macy's bed, clutching one of Macy's teddy bears. Trying to figure out a status update wasn't doing any good. Her daughter was gone...gone. It wasn't the time to play detective. Alyssa needed to get out there and find her daughter. She set the bear on a pillow.

She ran down to the front door, throwing it open without even taking the time to put on her shoes. She ran down the driveway, frost crunching under her socks. They started to get wet, but she didn't care.

Willis from across the street was out in his front yard, doing some yard work. Alyssa ran to him.

He looked up, appearing shocked. "Alyssa. Are you okay?"

"Have you seen Macy?"

"Not this morning. Is everything—?"

"No! No, it's not." She felt like her throat was closing up. "If you see her, bring her home."

"What's going on? Can I help?" Willis asked.

"She's missing!" Tears spilled out onto her face. Admitting it to someone she barely knew felt like defeat. "She's gone," Alyssa whispered. "I have to find her." She burst into a run, heading down the street.

As she ran in her socks, she stepped on a number of little sharp rocks. Failing to put on shoes now seemed like a stupid decision. She was only slowing herself down more when what she needed was speed. She had to talk to as many people as possible.

She saw another neighbor loading her kids into the car. Alyssa ran to them. "Jane, have you seen Macy?"

Jane shook her head and Alyssa ran off. She didn't have time to explain anything to anyone. What she needed was to find someone who had seen Macy.

Alyssa ran as fast as she could through the neighborhood, only stopping to ask anyone she saw if they had seen her daughter. It was a pretty tight-knit community, so at least everyone knew their family. She didn't have to deal with explaining what Macy looked like.

Finally, she circled back around to her house. No one had seen her. Of course they hadn't. Not if Macy had been gone since the night before. She ran back to her house and once inside, she pulled off her bloody socks and slid on some flip flops. Her feet burned and throbbed, but she didn't care. She had to get back out there.

"Where have you been?"

She turned around to see Chad at the top of the stairs. "I've been out looking for Macy. What have you been doing?"

"I've been on the phone, talking to everyone under the sun who's seen Macy's status update." Chad's eyebrows came together.

Alyssa ran her hands through her sweaty hair. "Okay. You keep talking to them. I'm going to talk to more neighbors. Someone has to know something."

He folded his arms. "We need to call the cops."

She leaned against the wall. "You're right. They can get more done than we can. You do that while I keep looking for her."

The corners of Chad's lips turned downward. "She's not out there. She's with some kid she met online, giving us a very public middle finger. This is her way of trying to let us—"

"Stop! I don't care what she did, Chad. I need to find our daughter. Call the cops—please."

"And have them take her downtown," he muttered. "That'll teach her."

Alyssa stared at him, unable to find words. Had she really heard him correctly? She didn't have time to argue with him. He'd been such a jerk lately, and this wasn't the time to try to change that. "Just call them."

She ran out the door again. Her feet ached more as the drying blood stuck to the flip flops. "Macy!" She looked around. Maybe if Macy was around hiding and saw how upset Alyssa was, she might come out of hiding. “Macy!”

This time, she ran to the park. Families were already gathering there. She screamed for Macy the entire way. Who cared if anyone thought she was crazy? She needed to get as many people looking for Macy as possible. She couldn’t do this on her own.

Dungeon

HER CAPTOR SHOVED Macy toward the hole in the barn's floor. She pushed against him, trying to stop him. She didn't want to go down there. She didn't even want to know what could be there.

"Are you testing me?" he growled. "Climb the ladder before I have to throw you down. You'll break a bone—I guarantee it."

"What's down there?"

"It's only a storm shelter. Get in!" He shoved her with more force.

She gulped and let go of him. He still squeezed her arm, but she lowered herself to the ground and stuck her feet down the hole. She had to feel around before finding the ladder. It was made of rope, and swung as she tried to steady herself. As soon as she was on her way down, he let go of her. Once her head was all the way below, he slammed the door shut over her. She could hear him moving the hay around over the door. Something clicked. A lock?

Macy stared up at the closed door above her until she felt a crick in her neck. Her eyes started to adjust to the light. She looked down and saw a few bales of hay. Sunlight shone in through walls of packed dirt.

Unsure of how long the ladder would hold her weight, she climbed down and put her feet on the dirt floor. She looked around. Everything was dirt. She walked around the square little storm cellar. It was a relief to see that it wasn't a torture chamber like she had feared. It was only a dirt cell with hay.

The hay actually helped it to smell a little better. It was musty, but the almost-sweet scent of the hay made it bearable. She sat on a stack of two bales and looked up at the light, watching the dust dance around for a little while.

She had to think of a way out.

But even if she were to stack all of the bales on top of each other, she wouldn't be able to reach the boards by the ceiling.

At least she was away from that psycho. Being alone was much better than being around him.

Her stomach rumbled. It was finally steady enough to be hungry again, but she had no desire to eat. Whatever he would give her, if he was going to give her anything else at all, would probably only give her more problems. She kicked her feet against the hay several times and looked around the room.

The wood at the top, near the ceiling, was old and cracking. Maybe she could pull the boards off piece by piece, if only she could reach them.

The dirt walls were dry, but not crumbling. Maybe she could find a way to make a ladder or steps in them if she could find something to dig the holes. It wasn't likely, but at least it was an idea.

Something squeaked. A rodent. How did it stay alive? Was there something to eat? Not that she wanted to eat mouse food, but it might come to that. She shuddered at the thought.

How much worse was this going to get? Macy didn't want to know. She jumped off the hay and climbed up the ladder as fast as she could. It swung every time she moved.

Holding on as tight as she could, she managed to get to the top without losing her footing. She pushed her foot into a corner of the walls, steadying herself once the ladder held still. Letting go of one hand, she pushed on the trap door. It didn't budge, so she pushed a few more times. She may as well have tried to rip off the whole ceiling.

Macy wrapped her leg in the ladder and braced with her other foot. Letting go of the rope, she pushed with both hands and all of her might. She ignored the rope as it swung again, but on her third push she lost her balance. As she fell upside down, her foot caught in the rope and anchored her in place.

Macy breathed a sigh of relief, glad to have not broken her neck. She grabbed onto the rope, grateful no one could see her as she hung upside down, feeling ridiculous. She was probably stupid for thinking she could get the door open.

Holding on, still upside down, she tried to pull her foot loose. It was stuck. Making sure not to let go, she pulled herself up little by little until she could reach her foot. With one hand, she pulled her foot free. It slid loose, and she maneuvered herself back into an upright position before climbing down.

Once on the ground, she looked around the room again. The rodents stayed out of sight. All she had left were the boards near the ceiling. They were well out of reach, but she had to try. She had to do something.

She went to one of the bales of hay, bent down, and pushed. It moved, but not much. It was a lot heavier than it looked. But what else was she going to do? Watch TV?

Sweat beaded on her skin as she pushed the bale again and again. Finally, it reached the wall, and she sat down on the hay to rest. It felt good to get a little exercise. Her muscles burned a little.

She was thirsty. When was the last time she had anything to drink? Not wanting to stop for long, she picked another bale, and pushed it toward the first one.

By the time she had the two bales against each other, she was wiping sweat from her eyes. How was she going to lift the second one on top of the first? She would have to wait; she didn't have the energy to try yet. She lay down on top of the two bales, imagining she was on a bed.

Something poked into her back. Macy sat up and saw something shiny in the bale. She pulled out what appeared to be a tube of lipstick. She pulled the top off to find exactly that.

Why was there makeup in the hay? She tossed it on the floor and lay down again.

Macy shivered, starting to get cold. As she readjusted her position, she noticed that the hay below her had grown warm. Maybe she could use it to hold heat. She sat up and dug her fingers into the hay, pulling out as much as she could, earning several scratches. That didn't matter. When she had a nice pile, she lay back down, and pulled as much of it over herself as possible, using it like a blanket.

It didn't take long to warm up. She closed her eyes, allowing herself to rest. She could hear hooves moving around above her. She hoped the ceiling was strong. The last thing she wanted to deal with was a cow or horse falling on top of her.

Guilt

ZOEY CARTER CLOSED her laptop in frustration. She had spent the last two hours searching for anything she could find on that Jared guy. It was as if he had ceased to exist. That wasn't possible—she had chatted with him. She could still remember his photo: an adorable selfie taken at one of his baseball games.

He was so sweet and had wanted to know what Macy liked. Jared had been so excited about their upcoming date, and had had a million questions. He didn't want to mess anything up, and Zoey had been more than happy to help him out. Macy had never had a boyfriend or gone on a date or anything. Her dad was so over-protective; he wouldn't let her do anything.

He wouldn't even let her watch PG-13 movies until she turned thirteen. Zoey always made sure they watched the good ones at her house so Macy could see what everyone else was seeing. Kids were always making fun of her, and Zoey didn't want to give them another reason.

The door opened, and her mom came in. "Has anyone heard from Macy yet?"

"No." Zoey frowned, fighting tears. "She's going to be okay, isn't she?"

Her mom walked over and wrapped her in a hug. "I sure hope so."

"But she would have called me. Why hasn't she texted or anything?"

"Well, her wall post sounds pretty upset. If she really wants to get to her parents, she would stay away from contacting you because she'd know they would call you first."

"Still, she should let me know if she's okay. She should know I can keep a secret."

"You know in a case like this, it's more important to break secrets, right?" Her mom raised an eyebrow.

Zoey rolled her eyes. "Of course. But she should tell me, you know?"

The landline rang.

Her mom gave her another hug. "I'd better get that. Maybe it's news about Macy."

Twirling a strand of jet-black hair, Zoey looked around her room. There had to be something she was forgetting. Something that would give an important clue. There was no way Macy had run away. If anyone would have seen it coming, it would have been Zoey. They told each other everything. Well, almost everything. There was that one thing she hadn't told Macy.

Macy had been looking forward to that date so bad. It was all she had talked about for the last week. She spent more time planning what to wear than she did on anything else. She was as excited about sneaking out as she was about going on a date with Jared. She had been tired of being a goody two-shoes, and couldn't wait to prove she wasn't anymore.

She spun around in her chair, looking at all the things that reminded her of Macy. *Would* Macy have run away with Jared? To spite her parents?

Had the thrill of sneaking out with Jared been enough to unlock her wild, crazy side? Was that why she took off with him? A smile tugged at Zoey's mouth. Maybe that was it. This could have been a loud, defining moment for Macy. Think of the fun times they could have when she came back, assuming her parents got the message and finally gave her some permission to have fun. They were probably going crazy right now not knowing where Macy was.

Zoey's mom came back into the room. "I'm sorry to do this to you, but we have to go down to the police station."

"What? Why?" Zoey felt like she had been punched in the gut.

"The police want to question anyone who could know anything about Macy's disappearance."

Zoey ran her hands through the length of her hair. "Isn't there a twenty-four hour wait or something? She ran away, didn't she?"

"The police aren't assuming anything. She met with someone online that nobody can even locate. They want to eliminate all possibilities."

"Wait. You mean they think she might have been kidnapped?"

"Nobody knows. There are a lot of child predators out there. That's why I'm always telling you not to give out any personal information."

Zoey took a deep breath. "But I talked with Jared. He was nice. I saw his picture."

"Did you ever meet him?"

She shook her head.

"If you want to help Macy, we need to go downtown."

"Can I have a few minutes to get ready?"

"Sure, sweetie." Her mom squeezed her shoulder and left the room.

Zoey closed her door, then put her ear to it to make sure her mom really had walked away. She grabbed her jacket and slipped it on, opened her window, and climbed out onto the ledge. She looked at the woods that faced her back yard. Could Macy actually have been taken by some pedophile?

Zoey stuck her hand into her pocket, grabbed a box and pulled out a cigarette. She lit it and took a puff, holding it in for a moment. Letting her breath out slowly, she tried to relax.

She'd started smoking to look cool around the new kids she'd been hanging out with, but now she actually felt like she needed one. If her mom knew she was smoking, she would have a fit.

The last thing Zoey wanted was go to the police station. What if she said something that could get Macy into trouble? What if she got herself into trouble? Could they charge her with something because she knew her friend was going to sneak out? By law, she was only a kid.

Her heart sped up as she thought about different kinds of worst-case scenarios. What if they sent her to juvie? What if everyone hated her for keeping Jared a secret? She didn't let her mind go to the absolute worst case—something actually happening to Macy.

As much as she didn't want to admit it, deep down she thought that might be the most realistic option. If Macy had planned to run away with Jared, she'd tell Zoey and not post it for everyone.

Zoey took another drag.

Guilt punched her in the gut again as she thought about the other secret she was keeping from Macy—the one far worse than smoking.

What if Macy had found out about that? Would that have been enough to send her over the edge to run away?

Zoey took one last drag, then smashed the cigarette into the roof tile next to her. She needed another one, maybe the whole pack, but there wasn't time for that. She climbed back into her room and sprayed some air freshener. Then she opened her door and listened for her mom. She could hear her downstairs, talking on the phone.

Zoey grabbed some clothes and ran to the bathroom for a quick shower. What should she tell the cops? She should probably stick to Jared and what little she knew about him. She kicked herself for not downloading his picture.

Maybe one of Macy's other friends had talked with Jared and had been smart enough to save the picture.

Zoey got out of the shower and brushed her teeth to get rid of the last evidence of her new habit. She looked in the mirror, examining her teeth, and then she brushed her long, black hair. She promised herself that the next time she saw Macy, she would come clean. She would tell her everything. The thought that she'd caused Macy to run away ate at her.

There was a knock on the door. "Are you ready yet, Zoey? They're expecting us at the station."

"Hold on!" Zoey grabbed her black eyeliner. She gave her eyes a smoky look before putting on some mascara. She loved her exotic eyes. They were so dark and mysterious, thanks to her dad's Japanese roots.

Her mom drove her to the station in near-silence. Zoey really didn't want to talk about anything, and her mom usually respected that.

When they pulled into a parking spot, her mom turned to her. "Just tell them everything you know. Don't be nervous, okay? You're not in trouble. Everyone just wants to find Macy. You're her best friend, and you might know something that no one else does."

Zoey nodded. "Sure, Mom." She got out of the car, not wanting to talk about it any more.

They walked into the station together. Her mom told the officer at the front desk why they were there, and he filled out some paperwork. Then he looked up at Zoey's mom and then back to Zoey.

"Are you adopted?"

Zoey rolled her eyes. If she had a dollar for every time some ignorant bonehead asked that, she would be rich. Because she looked so much like her dad, everyone assumed she couldn't be related to her fair-skinned, auburn-haired mom. "My dad is Japanese."

The buffoon looked around. "Where is he?"

Zoey narrowed her eyes. "Isn't that the million-dollar question? Probably Japan, but who knows? If you figure it out, let me know."

He raised his eyebrows. "Okay. Unknown." He scribbled more on his paper. "You two can have a seat over there." He indicated toward the waiting area.

Zoey followed her mom to the chairs. Her heart raced as she looked around at the plain, white walls and numerous windows. Yelling came from somewhere down a hall.

Just as she was getting ready to jump from her seat and run back to the car, she heard familiar voices. She looked up to see Macy's parents and brother walking out from behind the main desk. They must have been questioned. Her mom and dad stopped at the desk and talked with the loser filling out paperwork.

Zoey's mom went up and gave Macy's mom a hug. Alyssa burst into tears, and the women held each other. "Oh, Valerie. I can't believe this is happening."

Zoey looked away, afraid of crying herself.

Alex sat down next her. His eyes were red and puffy.

"You okay?" Zoey asked, feeling stupid. Of course he wasn't.

"They have, like, a million questions. They're acting like Macy's dead." He shook his head and took a deep breath.

"She's fine. You know how tough she is. I'm sure it's like her update said. She wanted to get away from everything."

Alex shrugged. He looked into her eyes but said nothing.

Zoey looked over at their parents. They were talking with each other, paying no attention to the two kids. She put her hand on top of Alex's. He flipped his hand over and laced his fingers through hers.

"I don't know what I'll do if anything happened to her." He cleared his throat. "I couldn't—I mean, what would I do?" His eyes shone with tears.

"She's going to be okay." She squeezed his hand. "She is. You know what? She's probably off having the time of her life with Jared, with no clue what she's putting us through."

He nodded. "I hope. When she gets back, I'm gonna beat the crap out of her."

"Alex. We're leaving," Chad called.

He squeezed her hand before standing. They held their eye contact, their fingers lingering also. Before Alex reached his parents, he mouthed, "Call me."

Zoey nodded.

Identity

A THUD WOKE Macy up. She opened her eyes, confused.

"I see you've made yourself comfortable."

The trap door was open, and she could see her captor staring down at her.

"Do you want something to eat?"

She sat up, nodding. "And something to drink."

He laughed. "I'll bet you're thirsty after moving those bales around. I'll get you something, but you have to do one thing for me, Heather."

Heather?

"What?"

"Call me Dad."

Dad? Had he lost his mind? Then she remembered in the truck, he said something about her looking like his Heather. "Why?"

"Because, Heather. I'm your dad. I need to hear you call me Dad."

"Tell me your real name and I'll think about it."

He glared at her. "You know my name, Heather. It's Chester Woodran."

Chester? His name was *Chester*? No wonder he was such a jerk. With a name like that, he'd have to be mean to get any respect.

"Well?" He narrowed his eyes.

"You're not my dad! And I'm not Heather."

He shook his head. "See. That's exactly why I need you to call me Dad. As soon as you do, you'll get your food and water. One more chance."

"Never."

"I'll come back and see how agreeable you are later." The trap door slammed shut, and she heard the same click as before.

Was that why Chester had taken her? Had something happened to Heather, and he was trying to use Macy to replace the girl? If he thought she was going to call him Dad, he had another think coming.

Tears poked at her eyes as she thought about her family. Did they know she was missing? She wasn't sure how long she'd been gone, but since she had sneaked out of the house, they wouldn't have found out until the morning. Maybe not even late morning, if it was one of those days when her parents let her sleep in.

Even if they did know she was gone, would they know where to look for her? She had to be several states away, if not more. Would her friends have figured out that something was wrong? She had told her closest friends she was meeting Jared. Would they be worried that she hadn't texted them about it?

Burying herself further into the bed of hay, she gave in to the tears until she was sobbing and shaking. Where were her parents? What were they doing? What about her annoying brother? What she wouldn't give to even see him and put up with his relentless teasing.

Without realizing it, she cried herself back to sleep. She woke up when something tickled her hand, which was hanging out of the hay. She opened her eyes to find a black beetle crawling on her hand.

"Augh! Get off. Off of me!"

She shook her hand, but it didn't come loose. She used her other hand to flick it away. She wiped the back of her hand on the hay furiously, as though that would get rid of whatever remnants of the bug were left on her skin.

Was she going to die in this room? Was this going to be the last place she was ever going to see? Sleeping in hay with bugs crawling on her, surrounded by rats and who knew what else?

A loud crack made her jump. Macy buried herself deeper into the bale of hay, even though she knew it couldn't protect her. Rain slammed against the barn with such force that it practically shook above her. Thunder clapped again, and with it rainwater came dripping down the wall next to her. It pooled noisily on the ground.

Did it flood down there? The rats weren't running for cover, so maybe—hopefully—that was a good sign. She could hear animals stomping around up above. They whinnied, mooed, and bahhed, making the storm even more eerie than it already was.

Macy lay there in her hay nest, listening to the sounds of the storm and of the animals. It was the distraction she needed, and finally she relaxed for the first time since the ordeal had begun. Storms had always been somewhat comforting, in a strange sort of way. At home, she used to love watching the rainfall from her house. It was almost magical, even though she was too old to believe in that stuff anymore.

The storm gave her hope, almost like a sign she was going to be okay.

Her stomach rumbled along with the thunder and the hunger ate at her, making her feel weak and light-headed. She had been hungry before and knew this phase would pass. There was no way she was going to let him win. If nothing else, she would walk away from this skinny at last.

Focusing on the storm, she ignored the hunger pangs. She thought of her poor old cat Snowflake. Imagining him beside her helped Macy relax further. He had always been able to sense when she was upset, and would show up to comfort her.

As suddenly as it had begun, the storm stopped. The quiet rang in her ears, and all she could hear was the water dripping down the wall from the spaces above. Macy closed her eyes. She wanted sleep to take her away again, but it wouldn't.

Her stomach growled again, rumbling over and over, making her light-headedness even worse. Her mouth watered for food that didn't exist.

At home, she could walk into the kitchen and grab anything—well, anything without meat or animal by-products. Alex always waved cheese slices in her face after she declared herself a vegan. Cheese had been her favorite, and was probably the sole cause of her muffin top.

A noise caught Macy's attention, and she looked toward the trap door as it opened.

"Did you enjoy the storm? I was watching it by the fire, listening to music while lunch cooked in the oven. How did you like it from in here, Heather?"

"My name isn't Heather."

"The sooner you come to terms with the fact that you're Heather, the sooner you'll be able to get out of here. For now, are you ready for some food?"

"I'm not calling you *dad*."

"That's a shame. I've got some food here for you. Can you smell it?" Chester waved his hands around, like that would send the smell her way.

"Nope."

"Are you sure you won't change your mind?"

"I'm not Heather, and you're not my dad. I want you to take me back to my parents. Everyone's looking for me, you know. They've figured out by now that I'm missing. They'll find you."

"Don't count on that, Heather."

"They know something's wrong."

He shook his head. "You posted a note online, telling everyone of your intention to run away."

"What?" She sat up.

"You didn't think I could figure out those passwords, either?" He laughed. "Snowflake415. Your precious kitty and the date you decided to become vegan."

Macy gasped. "They'll still look for me. Even if I said I was running away." She clenched her fists. Would they, really? They had to. Her parents wouldn't shrug their shoulders and carry on with life if she ran away.

"Your note said not to look for you, that you would come back when you were ready."

She tightened her grip, digging her nails into her own flesh. "They won't believe it."

"I think they will. I know all your typical typos, your lingo, and all the chat-speak. They'll have no reason to doubt you wrote it from your own account."

He'd thought of everything. Even so, there was no way everyone would sit around, was there? She was a kid. The police would be forced to look for her, wouldn't they? Or did they not bother with runaways? Not that they would know to look for her below a barn in the middle of nowhere, probably states away.

"So, Heather, are you ready for lunch? I made you some vegetable soup—vegan approved."

Macy's stomach growled again, and her mouth filled with water. She couldn't let him know how much she wanted the soup.

"I'm not calling you dad. You're not my dad."

"Eventually, you'll be hungry enough to be agreeable. I thought you'd be now, but it looks like you'll need some more time. I'll leave the bowl up here and you can think about it while I go to the store. I might make some other stops too. Come to think of it, I might be gone for quite a while. Are you sure you don't want to eat now?"

She wanted to eat it more than anything, but there was no way she was letting him know that. "I'm fine. If you know me so well, you know how I lost my weight. I can go a long time without eating."

"Suit yourself. You're only human. Oh, that reminds me." He held a bottle of water. "You'll at least need something to drink if you're going to survive. You may be able to go a long time without food, but you can't go long without this. Drink it." Chester dropped it, and as it bounced on the dirt floor, he slammed the trap door shut and locked it.

Her mouth watered at the thought of the soup, reminding her how parched she was. He was right, and she knew it. She needed water. Macy climbed out of her little nest and ran to the bottle of water, picked it up, and stared at it. It was still factory sealed. There weren't any punctures in it anywhere.

Why had he given that to her? She told him she would never call him dad. Was he not planning on killing her? Did he want her to live? If that was the case, what was his plan? Did he actually want her to become his daughter? Like that would ever happen.

She twisted the cap off and guzzled the entire bottle. She put the lid back on and threw it into a corner.

In the distance, she heard an engine start, followed by tires driving on gravel.

Sneaking

ALEX SPRAWLED OUT across his messy bed, playing games on his cell phone and trying to distract himself from how stressed and worried he was. It didn't fix anything, but at least he could get his mind off Macy for a little while.

As if it wasn't bad enough that Macy had taken off—or been killed, by the sounds of what the police thought—he and his parents had been questioned. Zoey, too. She had to be as worried as he was. She'd been besties with Macy for as long has he could remember.

He moved up a level in Factoryville, and then chucked his phone across the room. He didn't care about any of the games. Not now. The police had said they were going to go through Macy's room if she didn't turn up soon, and told them not to leave town. Where would they go? Jerks.

Rolling over onto his back, he stared at a poster of his favorite band on the ceiling. When would Zoey call? It felt like forever since he saw her at the station. He hoped she was okay. She seemed about as well as could be expected, but that was before talking with the cops.

Alex's parents had been in the room when he was questioned, since he was a minor. The same should hold true for Zoey. He would feel a lot better being able to talk with her.

If they could talk, maybe they could figure out what really happened. What two people were closer to Macy, really? Sure, Macy and Alex didn't spill their secrets to each other, but they were pretty close. That was why she put up with his teasing. It was their thing. Always had been.

The doorbell rang, and Alex groaned. Let it be Zoey, and not the cops. He could tell by the way they looked at him that they didn't like him. His hair was past his ears, and he liked it scraggly. The older cop seemed to have him pegged as a thug. Did he seriously suspect that Alex had anything to do with it? That was ridiculous.

Opening his door, Alex could hear muffled conversation downstairs. At least it was a break from his parents arguing. They didn't get along anymore since Dad had started that blog. People online started thinking his dad was all that, so his head got big and he walked around upset that he didn't get the same respect at home.

Alex thought about closing his door to continue hiding, but he wanted to find out what was going on. Maybe the police had found something. Macy's picture was all over the TV. Every discussion on social media was about her, too. That's why Alex had been playing games—he didn't want to read any more crazy theories. His friends had come up with everything from alien abduction to witness protection.

If Alex didn't stay away, he would end up beating the crap out of half the student body on Monday. Let them talk, but he wasn't going to have anything to do with it. He made his way downstairs and saw his parents talking with three cops. One officer he hadn't seen at the station tipped his hat. Alex nodded back and stood a distance away, not wanting to be dragged into the conversation.

It didn't sound as though they had anything new to share.

"We need to search the house and we need you to step outside while we do," said the one who had given Alex the evil eye back at the station.

"What?" Alex exclaimed. He looked at his parents, begging them to say no. "Why do we have to leave? We didn't do anything wrong."

Hat-tipper looked at him. "Then you have nothing to worry about, son. We should be in and out of here in no time. If there are any clues to your sister's disappearance, then we need to find them sooner rather than later. The first twenty-four hours are critical."

Alex frowned. "Can I go back and get my cell phone?"

Jerkwad shook his head. "No can do. You can have it back when we're done. Now, please step out of the house."

"Fine." Alex walked past his parents and the cops, out the door.

Alyssa looked at him. "You can put your shoes on."

He glared at the jerk cop. "Wouldn't want to interfere with the investigation."

Chad narrowed his eyes. "Alex, it's the middle of November. Put some shoes on. Why are you being like this?"

"Why? Because my sister is missing and we're being treated like criminals."

"That's how he expresses sorrow." Chad picked up a pair of flip-flops and flung them at Alex.

He caught them. "Awesome." After putting them on, Alex walked down their walkway. "Am I allowed to walk down the street?" He didn't wait for a response before making his way to the sidewalk. He looked down the street and saw Zoey's mom's car parked in front of their house, two doors down.

Before he even made it to their driveway, Zoey ran outside. "Sorry I didn't call you. My mom wouldn't stop talking to me. I swear, she needs to get married and leave me alone."

"That won't solve anything. Trust me."

"True. Your parents haven't been getting along lately."

"Want to go to the park? The cops are going through my house."

"That bites. We're probably next, though. Yeah, let's go there."

Alex grabbed her hand, and they walked the three blocks to the park in silence. They went to their typical hiding spot underneath a tree with many swooping branches and sat down against the trunk, hidden from the world. Zoey leaned her head against his chest.

"Where do you think she is?" asked Alex.

"I hope she's having a good time with Jared, but the fact that he's gotten rid of everything identifying worries me. Why would he do that? I went through the messages he sent me, and there's nothing in there about him. All he did was ask me about Macy and say how much he wanted to make her happy. The police even said that sounds really suspicious."

"They should try to get into his account."

Zoey looked at him. "They did. They called customer support and everything. He covered his tracks by hiding his IP address or whatever. I don't know all that lingo."

"So, basically, they have no idea where or who Jared is."

"Nope." She pulled out a cigarette. "Want one?"

"I'll share with you. Sorry I got you hooked."

"I'm not hooked. I can stop anytime. I think it'll take the edge off." She lit it, took a drag, and then handed it to him.

Alex took the longest, slowest drag he could manage. He wanted to make it last since they were sharing. He didn't want to admit how good it felt. He knew if his sister was there, she would be mad at both of them, especially for encouraging each other.

They sat in silence until the cigarette was gone. Alex shoved it into the ground, twisting it back and forth.

Zoey leaned back against him. "What do you think is going to happen?"

He shrugged. "At home, I keep expecting her to walk around the corner. I know she's not there, but I keep thinking she's going to. It's stupid."

"No, it's not. I keep waiting for her to text me or something. I keep wanting to call her, but then I remember I can't."

"Do you think Jared was real? Or some old creeper?"

"I don't think it was the kid in the picture. He looked too sweet and innocent to do anything wrong. You know, the kind of guy who would insist on opening her door, not talk her into running away."

"What if we never see her again?"

"It's too soon to think like that."

"But you said—"

"Remember all those positive thinking CDs your parents used to make us all listen to when we were kids? If there's any truth to them, what Macy needs is for us to thinking she's going to come back. She needs our positive thoughts. They'll reach her and help her."

"You really believe that crap?"

"I don't know. It seemed to work."

"Did you actually try?"

"Yeah. Maybe."

"It didn't help my family. My parents fight all the time and they pushed Macy away."

"But they don't listen to those anymore, do they?"

Alex shook his head.

Zoey took his hand and slid her fingers through his. "See? They got along when they did. Remember?"

"I guess."

"They did. I was jealous. Trust me."

He wrapped his arm around her and sighed. "This whole thing sucks balls."

"It's an effing nightmare. When she comes back, I'm going to give her a hug, then I'm gonna slap her across the face."

"You and me both."

"When she comes back, we really should tell her about us."

Alex looked at her in surprise. "You think so?"

"Well, yeah. I always feel bad about keeping it from her. I was afraid she'd hate me. But if she cares about us, she'll be happy for us. Then we could all hang out together. We won't have to hide from her."

"Your parents would never let you spend the night again. We wouldn't get easy make out sessions anymore."

"Who said anything about telling them?"

They sat for a while, watching the feet of people go by and listening to kids squeal and shout at each other. Alex thought back to when they were all kids. Zoey had practically grown up with him and Macy.

She had been like a sister to him his whole life until last summer. Somehow she'd started to seem different to him. Then one night, Macy fell asleep while they'd all been watching a scary movie. A frightening scene came on, and both Alex and Zoey screamed. They looked at each other and laughed, but when they made eye contact, something changed.

When the movie ended, they sat there on the couch, talking for hours. They stayed up until about four, discussing everything from what the scariest movie was to which Pokémon was the strongest. They laughed over old memories and talked about jerks at school. Then, heart pounding, Alex made the riskiest move of all. He leaned over and kissed her on the lips, not knowing if she would push him away or kiss back.

Zoey had kissed him back, surprising him with her passion. He had expected her to shove him on the floor and tell on him. They decided not to tell Macy—or anyone.

For some stupid reason, it was okay for guys to go out with girls two years younger, but girls couldn't. They had always planned on eventually coming clean to Macy. She deserved to know, and if anyone was going to figure them out it would have been her, but as far as they could tell, she was clueless. She definitely didn't know that when Alex snuck out, he was meeting with Zoey.

Zoey had been afraid to tell Macy and lose her best friend. Even though Alex and Macy bickered, she was quite protective of her little brother. She always had been. One time, a girl from school had been teasing Macy and she said some remark about Alex becoming sexy. That was the one time they had seen Macy get really pissed. She went off on that girl like nothing Alex had ever seen. He had thought for sure that Macy was going to deck the girl, but she had stormed off instead.

Macy wouldn't stand up for herself when it came to kids at school, but when someone said something about Alex, the inner monster had been released. Alex didn't want to have that turned on Zoey, and Zoey didn't want her lifelong best friend hating her.

Zoey sat up straight. "I can feel my phone vibrating. I'm sure Mom wants me back home."

"I should probably get back too. My parents are going to freak out and not let me go anywhere now that Macy's gone. My days of sneaking out are about to end. What are you going to say about smelling like smoke?"

She flipped her hair back. "The usual. I ran into kids smoking at the park."

He nodded and then kissed her, hoping she wouldn't get mad at him for kissing her while Macy was gone. Instead, she kissed him back, holding him tighter than usual. Her phone vibrated again, and he could feel it.

Zoey stood. "I should go before my mom has a nervous breakdown."

"Yeah. Me too."

She gave him a quick kiss and then walked away. He watched her until she disappeared from sight.

Anxiety

MACY LEANED AGAINST the bale of hay she had been pushing and wiped the sweat from her forehead. She was determined to pile them up so she could reach the wood near the ceiling. She had been staring it at it long enough. She knew that if she could reach it, she could pull the boards loose and squeeze through.

Sure, she didn't really have a plan beyond that. She didn't know how to get off the farm, or where to go once she reached a main road. She had to take everything one step at a time and the first thing was to get the bales piled on top of each other.

She looked around, searching for a way up to the boards before the madman came back. She didn't know how long he had been gone, but it felt like forever. He was bound to be back soon.

What did he have planned for her? Would he let her starve if she never caved and called him Dad? She didn't have the best relationship with her own dad, but she wasn't going to give in and disown him.

Too exhausted to even attempt pushing one of the heavy bales on top of another, she paced the room. As she thought about how she was going to get out, her mind wandered back home. Was anyone worried about her?

If that jerk was smart enough to remove her cell phone battery, there was no way anyone would ever find her. She remembered when her dad had gotten those phones. How could she forget? He had gone on for nearly an hour explaining how they would always know where she and Alex were with those. Macy and her brother had rolled their eyes at each other, both knowing they could leave their phones somewhere if they were going to sneak anywhere.

Not that Macy was one to sneak around. Her brother was the master of sneaking in and out. She knew he was seeing friends who smoked with him, but she wasn't about to tattle. He assured her that he wasn't doing any other drugs. She had told him that as long as he wasn't doing anything dangerous, she would keep their parents out of it.

Macy was sure if she ever got back home, she wouldn't sneak out again. At least not to meet someone she had never met before.

"Focus!" She shook her head. Thinking about all that wasn't going to help her get back home. Or even out of the barn.

She continued to pace in circles, staring at the bales of hay and the wood she was determined to peel away. As she walked, the room felt like it got smaller. She felt it might close in on her if she didn't do something soon.

With a sudden burst of determination, she ran at the nearest bale of hay and pushed on it as hard as she could from the bottom. It moved up into the air a couple of inches before dropping. Macy moved her fingers out of the way in time.

She balled up her fists and went to the other side of the room, startling the rodents. She narrowed her eyes at the bale and crouched down as though in a race.

"Ready. Set. Go." She ran at the hay and used her momentum to push it up. It went up farther but soon dropped down again. Not to be deterred, she returned to the other end of the room and repeated the imaginary race. She got the bale a little higher, but again, it dropped.

She repeated the process about five more times until she was too tired to try again. She lay down on the bale she had made a bed of and kicked her feet in frustration. She pounded on the wall next to her, not caring that it hurt her hands. She felt blood dripping down. All she had to do was pile up the hay and she could get out, but she couldn't even do that.

Light shone through the boards, mocking her. She pounded on the wall harder, so much so that little specks of dirt fell onto her, getting on her face. She wiped them away, and leaned against the wall. Hot, angry tears fell to her face, and she did nothing to stop them.

She let herself sob. Feeling the pain deep down in her gut, she let out a scream. She heard the animals move around above. She didn't care. She screamed again, that time louder.

"Why did I get into that truck? Why was I so stupid?" She got up, tears still pouring down her face, and kicked the hay. "And why won't you help me, you stupid bales?"

Macy reached down and pulled out pieces of hay, throwing them around herself. She grabbed more and threw them too. They came out easier where she had been kicking. She pulled out as many as would come and chucked them around the suffocating, little room. She let out another scream for good measure.

"Why? Why? Why?" She leaned against a wall and slid down until she was sitting on the ground. How had she been stupid enough to get herself into this situation? No one else she knew had been kidnapped. Only her. She had to be a special kind of stupid. It was no wonder no one at school ever wanted anything to do with her. In fact, the only guy who ever had any kind of an interest in her was a fake. He was a stalker. Some old dude, determined to turn her into his probably-dead daughter.

She put her head onto her knees and sobbed again. What was she going to do? Was there any possibility of her getting out? Even if she managed to get one bale on top of another, would she be able to get enough piled up to reach those boards?

And did it even matter? Her family would think she ran away. Maybe they would think she was happier without them. If Chester came back and killed her, it might be the best thing for everyone.

Face still on her knees, she continued to wail. What was the point of trying to get away? So she could go back to school and have everyone laugh at her and call her fat?

What was she fighting for, really? Was going back really so important? She could imagine the comments her "friends" were probably leaving on that post about her running away. They were probably telling her to stay away, saying good riddance. It was probably her most-liked post of all time.

Memories

ALYSSA STOOD BY the window in her bedroom, staring into the woods behind their house. She had run out of tears, but not grief. The longer Macy was missing, the more it ate away at her. She thought of the last thing she had said to her daughter the night before. It had been an irritated list of things for her to do over the weekend.

Why hadn't she given Macy a hug? Told her how much she loved her? A fresh lump formed in her throat. Sure, her kids annoyed her with their selfishness and lack of responsibility, but they were teenagers. Being moody and messy was practically in their job description. Alyssa hadn't forgotten being a teenager. Why couldn't she be more understanding? She had always promised herself that she wouldn't turn into her mom.

She was like her own kids in many ways, now that she thought about it. She was focused on her appearance, going to the gym daily. She was also busy distracting herself from the pain of the recent direction of her marriage.

Alyssa looked around her room. She missed the days when she and Chad would spend hours in there, talking and dreaming. If only he was there to hold her. Alyssa wanted to pour her heart out to him, but she couldn't even bring herself to leave the room and find him.

He had been in his study, avoiding her since they found out about Macy. He probably felt guilty—as he should. He was the one who had driven Macy to run away, if in fact that was what had happened.

Macy had to have snapped and run off, not wanting to be controlled any longer. Alyssa could remember hating control when she was a teenager. She had wanted so badly to be seen as an adult.

Her eyes landed on her old scrapbooks, sitting under a pile of other books. She hadn't looked at those in years. She walked over and picked them up, sliding the other books onto the shelf. She took the scrapbooks to the bed and opened the one that had Macy's baby pictures.

Alyssa couldn't help smiling at the memories in front of her. She needed to look at these more often to remind herself how much her kids meant to her. It was easy to forget when they threw their snarky attitudes at her, but seeing the old pictures made her heart swell with love. They were the same as they always had been, only bigger now, and rightfully wanting some independence.

She flipped through the pages until she couldn't keep her eyes open any longer. She gave into their heaviness and rested her head on top of one of the pages, giving into sleep.

Fear

MACY WATCHED THE rain drip down the wall next to her. She hadn't heard the truck return, and had no idea when Chester would be back. She was no longer hungry. She had spent so much time skipping meals that it got to the point where being hungry felt good.

Her stomach stopped rumbling while she was crying earlier, and she was grateful for some kind of pleasure. She wasn't sure how long the good feeling would last. Usually it went away when she saw or smelled food. The soup above was probably disgusting from sitting there so long, and knowing that helped her stomach to continue feeling good.

With every passing minute, she became less and less convinced she'd be able to get out. No matter how hard she tried, she couldn't get even one bale on top of another.

She thought about her brother. What did Alex think of her disappearance? He was so hard to read these days. They still got along, but they weren't close. It was as though something had come between them. His teasing bothered her more because of that, but she never said anything, not wanting to give him another reason to make fun of her.

He would be worried, though. It gave her comfort realizing that. Sure, he could be the most annoying kid on the planet, but he cared about her. He had been the first one to notice when she started starving herself. He had practically begged her to stop. Deep down, he was still the sweet kid he had always been.

She pulled more hay over herself and turned away from the wall. She could still hear water streaming down. It made her have to pee again, but she didn't want to get up. She'd wait until she couldn't hold it.

Was her best bet to pretend to be Heather? She really had no chance at escaping, unless the psycho moved her somewhere else. Why would he? He probably knew she wouldn't be able to get out.

Thunder cracked, and she jumped. She pulled more hay over herself, trying to hide from it.

If she pretended to be Heather, would he give her more freedom? An actual bed, maybe? Would he let her stay in the farmhouse with him? Obviously she wouldn't get her cell phone back, but lying in a bed sounded so nice. Maybe she would even get some fresh clothes.

Maybe if she pretended to be his daughter, he would be nice to her. What if he continued to be a jerk? What had happened to the real Heather, anyway? She could try to find out if he let her out of the basement. It was worse than being in jail. Prisoners at least had rights and meals. She had nothing.

Why was she even considering giving into him? That was what he wanted. She was down there so he could turn her into an obedient captive. Macy had taken psychology. That was exactly his plan. But maybe if she knew that, she would be able to keep herself from getting Stockholm's syndrome and becoming sympathetic to him.

He wouldn't really go back and kill her family. He was only playing her.

Macy needed a new plan, and unfortunately, that meant she was going to have to pretend to be his daughter. She would have to think of herself as a performer. The farm was her stage, that jerk was her audience. On the outside, she would be Heather, but on the inside, she would remain Macy.

She had to. It was her only real hope of escape.

Was the time passing slowly, or was that jerk staying away for a long time to mess with her? She rolled back over and looked up at the boards.

She had probably been dreaming, thinking she could actually get out on her own. Chester would have taken every measure to make sure she couldn't get out. He might have even put something in the bales to make them heavier.

Now that she wanted out, she wasn't sure what was worse: being alone in the horrid dungeon or pretending to be Heather and acting like Chester was her dad. She didn't even want to look at him, much less act like his kid, but it was her only hope of escape.

A noise outside caught her attention. At first, she thought it was the rumbling thunder again. Soon it sounded like wheels on gravel. Her heart picked up speed. Was he coming to check on her? Would she soon be climbing the rope ladder to never see the awful room again?

Macy held her breath, listening to the sound of crunching gravel. She sat up when she heard a slight squeal of brakes. She couldn't hear anything over the pounding of her heart.

"Please come in the barn," she whispered.

She took several deep breaths, trying to calm her racing heart. She heard a car door slam, followed by what sounded like footsteps over wet gravel. Soon, all she could hear was the rain. She held her breath, trying to hear more.

Something moved above her. She heard shuffling noises. Something clicked, and then creaked. Macy stared at the trap door, squeezing the hay in her hands.

The door opened, and after what seemed like forever, he put his face down where she could see it. "Looks like you've been busy. Did you throw a party while I was gone?" He laughed. "Did you have enough time to think about what we discussed?"

What they *discussed*? She stared at him, refusing to answer. She wanted to choose her words carefully. If she said the wrong thing, he might lock her up again.

"Not feeling talkative? I've got some things for you, if you're ready for them, Heather. We'll start with a vegan lemon and asparagus pasta. You can have a shower and put on your new clothes. It's the same outfit you wanted before we went on our trip. Do you remember? Try to forget about what happened to your mother. There's no sense in replaying that in your mind over and over."

What was he talking about?

"Do you remember what you have to say in order to get out of here, Heather?"

Macy clenched her fists. "Yes, Dad."

His eyes widened, and then he smiled. "Good. Good. I'm so glad to hear it, Heather. You get this place cleaned up, and I'll get everything ready." He slammed the door shut, and then Macy could hear the click of the lock.

She stared at the door in disbelief. He hadn't let her out? How much longer was she going to be down there? Tears filled her eyes, and she wiped them away before they could fall to her face.

What exactly did he mean by clean up? Did he only want her to pick up the hay she had thrown around? Or did he want her to put the bales back where they had been? Unable to bear the thought of spending any more time down there, she got up and started the process of moving the heavy bales back to their original positions. At one point, she slipped on the tube of lipstick.

Macy picked it up and examined it. It was an expensive brand. She recognized it as one that Zoey's mom liked to wear. It was strange that pricey makeup would be in a bale of hay in an underground cellar in the middle of nowhere. She didn't have the time or energy to figure out what it was doing there. She shoved it into the hay and continued to push the bale.

Angry tears filled her eyes as she pushed the hay around the room. What was it going to take to finally get out of the horrible, little room?

Her muscles burned from pushing the hay around. They weren't used to being used, and they protested. She had no other choice except to ignore them, right along with her stomach. The labor made her hungry again, and it didn't feel good in the slightest. Macy was getting dizzy, and beads of sweat broke out around her face.

Too tired to keep going, she stopped and leaned against the bale, breathing heavily. She tried listening for noises, hoping Chester would be back soon, but she couldn't hear anything over the sounds of her own heartbeat and her heavy breathing.

She noticed the individual pieces of hay she had thrown around the room. Sighing, she stood and picked up one after the other, stuffing them into the bale that had a dent from where she'd taken them, until there were no more left lying around on the floor. She looked around the room again, frustrated at how much more work she had to do to get the bales put back where they were originally.

Her legs and arms ached, as did her shoulders, back, and stomach.

The last thing she wanted to do was push them around anymore. Did she dare risk leaving them as they were? He would probably know most of them still weren't where they belonged.

Macy kicked the nearest bale, hurting her toe inside the shoe. It felt like everything hurt, and her stomach growled. Her throat was parched, with her tongue practically sticking to the roof of her mouth. She knew she couldn't move another bale, at least not until she either had some food or rest.

Perhaps she could beg him to let her eat before moving the rest of them. She needed something. Her aching muscles couldn't be denied any longer, so she threw herself on the hay, unable to take her body's pleas any longer. Her eyes closed on their own, and she didn't fight them. She half-listened to the mice.

The now-familiar sounds of the door in the ceiling caught Macy's attention. She looked up to the door and saw Chester.

"It looks much better down here. You're finally ready to come to the house with me."

Clean

MACY STUMBLED AS she walked through the field between the barn and the farmhouse. It felt good to stretch her legs, and she hadn't realized how stale the air in the cell had been until she got out into the fresh, country air. She gulped it, even though her lungs burned.

They walked in silence. Macy had so many questions, but didn't want to risk getting thrown back into the hay room. At least until she had some food, and maybe even a shower. Both sounded like luxuries.

When they reached the house, Chester opened the door without unlocking it. He indicated for her to go in first. She walked in without looking at him. Smells of cooking food assaulted her, making her feel hungrier and yet a little nauseated.

"Doesn't it feel good to be back at your grandparents' house?" He closed the door. "Some things never change, do they? I swear, this place is the same as when I grew up here." He looked her over. "They certainly wouldn't approve of how filthy you are. Let's get to your room and you can clean yourself up. I need to put the blackberry pie in the oven, anyway. Do you remember where your room is?"

Was he crazy? Macy shook her head, still not looking at him.

"I thought you might have forgotten. They're right. We need to visit more often. They miss their only grandchild. They're due back soon, so I'm glad you finally came around. I don't know how I would have explained you being in that barn." He shook his head. "Follow me."

He went past her, down the hall, and stopped in front of one of the last doors. "Does this ring any bells?"

Macy shook her head again, keeping her gaze off him.

"We're going to have to work on your memory. I'll have to pull out our old family albums. It might hurt to see pictures of your mom, especially after what happened. I know your grandparents are going to ask about her. We're going to tell them she decided to stay in Paris. Can you do that?"

She nodded.

"Say it."

Macy took a deep breath. "Mom stayed in Paris."

"Good." He opened the door, showing what was obviously the room of a teenage girl.

Macy's eyes lit up despite herself. It was gorgeous, and most importantly, the bed was huge and looked really comfortable.

"Find yourself some clothes, and I'll show you to the bathroom. You probably don't remember where that is, either." He sounded irritated, as though it was a huge inconvenience to give her the tour of a house she had never seen before.

She walked past him into the room. As her gaze passed over the two windows, she noted that they were bolted down. Had he turned the house into a prison, too?

Opening a drawer, she picked out a shirt. She went through the rest of them, until she had a complete outfit. She looked down at what she was wearing. The dirty clothes would probably have to be burned.

"You done yet?" He tapped his toes.

Macy nodded, still facing away from him. She turned around and left the room, following him to the bathroom. It had a large tub, without a shower. She was going to have to take a bath. She couldn't even remember the last time she had taken one.

"Towels and everything you need are in there. Try not to take too long, because the food will get cold soon. I know how much you hate cold food, Heather."

She cringed at being called Heather, but figured she would have to get used to it for the time being.

He closed the door, and she turned around and locked it. She looked at everything in the cozy little country bathroom. It was all exactly what she would expect from a farmhouse bathroom. She turned the water on, got it to a comfortable temperature and jammed the plug into the drain at the bottom.

Macy looked down at her clothes again. She would have to get rid of them, not only because they were dirty beyond cleaning, but also because the psycho certainly wouldn't let her hang onto anything from her real life. She had to peel everything off, as it was all sticking to her skin.

Macy threw everything into the garbage. She stepped into the tub, but immediately jumped out. The water burned her frigid skin. She checked it with her fingers, finding it to be fine. She would have to climb in and let her exhausted body adapt to the temperature.

Once she acclimated to the water, she scrubbed herself clean. She didn't want to waste any time. Chester was sure to become angry if she took her time.

When she put on the clean clothes, she found them to be exactly her size. He had really done his homework, finding someone who even wore the same size as Heather. If Macy hadn't lost all that weight, she'd be too big to replace Heather. Then she might not even be in this mess. In a way, this mess was the fault of those jerks at school.

Macy shook her head. It didn't matter now. For now, she needed to eat and then explore the house to see if there was a way out.

Once dressed, she dug through the drawers to find a brush. All she could find was a comb, and it didn't want to go through her hair. But after everything else she had been through, that was a minor inconvenience.

Looking in the mirror, she barely recognized herself. Her skin looked horrible, and she had dark circles under her eyes. Her stomach rumbled as she combed her hair into place as best as she could.

She rummaged through the drawers for makeup, but found none. Seriously? Nothing? Macy sighed. It probably didn't matter. Who was she trying to impress?

Macy hung the towel on a hook and took a deep breath. Now was the moment of truth. She was going to have to walk into the kitchen and face her abductor. Hopefully he would feed her without making her jump through any more hoops. Her stomach growled again. She could smell the cooking food, and it made her mouth water.

Turning the doorknob, she took another deep breath as she prepared herself for what would come. As she walked down the hall, she could hear a TV. It sounded like the evening news. They were talking about politics. Boring.

When she entered the kitchen, she saw two places set at the table. Her fake dad had his back to her, cooking something over the stove. She stood still, not wanting to alert him to her presence. She looked around the room, hoping to find a way of escape. Not that she expected to get away just yet—all she wanted was to eat, anyway. She would attempt to get away later, perhaps while he slept.

Finally, unable to take the smell of the food, she cleared her throat. He turned around. "Oh, good. You're all cleaned up. You must be starving. Sit down and eat. Tomorrow's a big day."

Macy raised an eyebrow. What did that mean? She didn't intend to stick around and find out. She would go along with him for the time being, but at night she could find a way to escape. Then she would never have to know what else was up his sleeve.

He laughed. "Don't seem so surprised, Heather. We need to get you ready to see your grandparents again. Sit and eat. I know you're hungry." He turned back to the stove.

She stared at the food on the table, the smells tempting her. Finally she walked to the table. As she pulled the chair out, her mouth watered enough that she had to swallow it to keep it from escaping.

Sitting, she stared at the pasta, the fruit salad, and the cornbread. She was so hungry that she wasn't even going to question what was in it. She'd already broken her vegan diet, who cared if the bread had milk or butter in it?

Piling the food on her plate, her hands shook from hunger. She stared at the full plate for a moment before picking up the fork.

Then she dug in, barely stopping to breathe as she emptied the plate. When she was done, she was surprised to see him sitting at the table, also eating.

He smiled at her. "So good to see you eating again, Heather. Have some more. I made it for you."

She held her face still. Would she get used to being called Heather? Now that she finally had some food, she wasn't going to complain.

"Tomorrow's a big day since you haven't seen your grandparents in so long. It's getting dark, so we'll get ready for bed soon."

Macy's heart skipped a beat. What did he mean by getting ready for bed? This nightmare wasn't going to get even worse, was it?

He set his glass down, and smiled again. "In case you forgot, my room is next to yours. So if you need anything tonight, that's where I'll be."

She let out a sigh of relief. It was bad enough that he was trying to convince her that she was his daughter, but at least that was all it was. At least he wasn't trying to make her into a wife.

"I'm not used to you being so quiet. Hopefully after a good night's sleep, we'll be able to pick up where we left off." He went back to eating.

Pick up from where? What had happened to the real Heather? Macy took the glass in front of her and drank it down. She looked at the food sitting on the table, but didn't dare take more, even though she could have eaten it all. Her stomach had been empty, so she had to take it easy or she would throw up, and he would make her clean it up again.

"Are you full?"

She nodded.

"You want dessert? I can save it for tomorrow. I know how much you like cold pie for breakfast."

Cold pie for breakfast? That sounded weird, but also good. She shrugged her shoulders. Then she went back to the bathroom, with her mind racing. As she brushed her teeth, ignoring the fact that the toothbrush was obviously not new, she decided to stay awake as long as possible. She would make her escape after he went to bed.

Communication

CHAD ENTERED THE bedroom, relieved to see Alyssa sleeping. He hadn't wanted to deal with her any more than he had to. The looks she shot him while they spoke with the cops told him that she blamed him for all of this. It wasn't his fault Macy had run off with that kid. He didn't tell her to do that. In fact, he had set up the rules to avoid exactly this.

He didn't buy the story the cops were trying to sell them. He'd been studying her online profiles, and Macy's latest status update was nothing more than her flipping the bird at him in front of the whole world, especially since the post was public. She was saying loud and clear that she wouldn't be controlled. At least that's what he hoped. He couldn't bring himself to think about the alternative.

Reading through the comments on her post, it looked like a lot of her friends agreed with him. They were begging her to come back, and some kids were even apologizing for making fun of her at school. Everyone but the police and his family thought she was off having fun, and probably checking her account to see everyone's reactions.

Chad sat down next to Alyssa and picked up one of the photo albums. It opened to a page full of pictures of a camping trip they'd taken when the kids were younger. They all looked so happy roasting marshmallows. There was even a picture of him kissing Alyssa. A smile crept across his face as he remembered Macy snatching the camera and taking the picture, giggling and teasing them.

He set the scrapbook down and ran his fingers over Alyssa's hair. What had happened to them? They had been high school sweethearts, and each other's first love. Neither one had ever even gone on a date with anyone else. Maybe that was the problem. They knew each other too well.

There was no more mystery or magic.

Only laundry and errands.

Chad had thought that would improve once Alyssa stopped working. Instead, the house was no cleaner, and they argued more. Apparently, not working only magnified the fact that he was so busy. It gave her more time to fret and fuss about them not spending as much time together as they used to.

Didn't she understand that it wouldn't last forever? Once he made enough with his blog to support the family, he would be able to quit his job. He could work on his blog at night and they could have the days to spend together. Or he could work during the day, and they could have long romantic evenings like they used to.

Alyssa stirred in her sleep. He brushed some hair away from her face. Her eyes opened and a look of surprise covered her face—but he saw none of her usual disdain.

"Shh." He moved some of her hair behind her ear. Looking at her ear, he remembered how much he used to love nibbling on it and making her giggle. He ran a finger along it. He looked back to her face, surprised to see her looking directly into his eyes.

"What are we going to do, Chad?" Tears shone in her eyes.

His heart nearly leapt out of his chest. He felt like he was young again, when he would have done anything to keep her from hurting. He pulled her up and held her in his arms. She shook and he rubbed her back, whispering that everything would be okay. He expected her to snap at him that he didn't know that, but she didn't.

Chad knew he should say something. If only his parents were alive. Oh how he missed being able to talk to them. His dad always knew the right thing to say.

Finally, she leaned back and looked at him again. "I don't know what I'll do if—"

Chad put a finger to her lips. "We can't think like that. We can't let ourselves go there. She just ran away, like her status update says, and then she'll be back."

"We don't know that. Don't we need to prepare ourselves in case…?"

"Remember those CDs you used to make us listen to? We have to think positive."

Alyssa frowned.

"If the cops are right and Macy is in trouble—which I don't think is the case—then we need to do what we can to help her."

"Do you really believe that?" Alyssa asked.

"You don't?"

"Haven't you noticed I threw those CDs out?"

"Of course. You still know what was on them. We all do."

Alyssa's cell phone rang, and she glanced at it. "It looks like Sherry from down the street. I'm so tired of talking on the phone. I only want to leave it on in case Macy tries to call." She pushed ignore.

Chad nodded. "Between my phone and the land line, I'm ready to smash them all."

"If it weren't for the chance of Macy calling, I would join you."

He smiled. "Could you imagine that? Us running around, destroying the phones?"

One corner of Alyssa's mouth curled up. "That would be quite a sight."

Chad's phone rang. "We could always start now. I've been wanting to upgrade anyway."

She shook her head. "Who's calling now?"

He looked at his phone. "Sherry again."

"Maybe we should answer. What if it's important?"

Chad handed her his phone.

Alyssa rolled her eyes, but took it anyway. "Sherry?"

"Hi, Alyssa. I'm sorry to bother you, and I won't keep you. I want to let you know that a bunch of the kids from the high school put together a candlelight service at the park near your house. It's supposed to start around seven. Then in the morning, there's going to be a rally. Missing posters have been printing all day and people are going to hand them out."

Alyssa stared into space, trying to take it all in. "I'm a terrible mother."

Chad gave her a questioning look.

"What do you mean?" Sherry asked. "Of course you're a wonderful mom."

"I should have been the one to put all that stuff together. I've been sitting around feeling sorry for myself."

"You're doing everything you can. You've been talking with the police and everything, dear. The community wants to rally around you. The news keeps talking about the worst, but the good news is that everyone is banding together. Everyone wants to help Macy return safely."

"Thanks, Sherry. Where's the rally?"

"Everyone is meeting at the high school around eight in the morning. You guys don't need to show up, but I think the support would really help."

"Of course we'll help. We'll be at the front of the line."

"We'll see you tonight. Just to let you know, the news media will probably be there."

"Good. The more coverage, the better. Thanks, Sherry." Alyssa ended the call and looked at Chad.

"What's going on?"

She repeated everything Sherry had told her, barely getting through without tears.

Chad held her again. "We'll get through all of this—and of course you're not a bad mom. How could you say that? You're the best mom around."

Alyssa couldn't hold the tears in any longer. She buried her face in his chest and sobbed.

The broken look on her face made him want to make everything right again. He kissed the top of her head and held her until she calmed down. "We've done what we could. Dealing with the police has been time consuming and stressful. They're being nice enough, but still treating us like we could be criminals. Family is always the first suspect."

"They need to get out there and find *Macy*."

"Between the fliers and the news coverage, everyone is going to know what Macy looks like, and hopefully someone will see her. When they do, they'll recognize her immediately."

"I hope she didn't get kidnapped. Do you think that's what happened?"

"I've been staring at that status update, and it sounded exactly like her. They say a predator could have forced her to log in and write that, but I don't know what to think. I've been so sure she was flipping us a giant bird for all to see, but with each passing hour, I start to doubt a bit more. She wouldn't be gone this long on purpose, would she?"

Alyssa shook again, more tears falling down her face. "It's not like her. She always threatens us before she does something. Even before going vegan, remember? She told us several times if we didn't start making healthier meals, she was going to follow the Hollywood trend and get skinny like the actors."

"I don't want to think about her being abducted. I can't." Chad blinked away tears of his own. "Teenagers are impulsive. They don't think anything through. She's been complaining that I let Alex get away with murder. She may have decided to stick it to me, and now she's afraid to come back, knowing I'll ground her."

"We need to give her more freedom. We have to. She's right. Her younger brother can do more than her."

Chad took a deep breath. "I don't want to have this argument now. We need to stick together. I don't know about you, but I can't make it through this, living at odds like we have been."

Alyssa looked like she was going to say something, but nodded instead. Chad moved the scrapbooks out of the way. "Let's get some rest before the rally." He grabbed his phone. "What time should I set the alarm?"

"Six."

He got comfortable and extended his arm. She crawled next to him and for the first time in a long while, they fell asleep in each other's arms.

Thwarted

MACY SAT IN the bed, listening for sounds of her fake dad going to bed. She could hear a sitcom, and every once in a while, his laughter. She didn't want to lie down—if her head felt the pillow, she knew she would be asleep right away.

It had already been two hours. When was he going to go to bed? She yawned, unable to deny how tired she was. Sleeping in a bale of hay had been almost as bad as not sleeping at all. Sleeping in the truck had been even worse.

She could hear music, and it sounded like a new show starting. Maybe he was staying up on purpose—to keep her inside. His laughter drifted in through the door along with canned laughter from the sitcom, as though in response to her thoughts.

Perhaps sleep was her best option, at least for the time being. Maybe it would take a couple of days for him to trust her enough for her to get away.

Giving into her heavy eyes, she set the alarm for eight, figuring that would be enough time. She wouldn't need a shower, and the cold pie would already be ready.

She dug through the drawers for some pajamas. At least Heather had comfortable ones.

Who was Heather, anyway? Aside from being his daughter, of course. Being in her room, Macy had a feel for the kinds of things she liked, but still knew nothing about her. Most importantly, where was she?

It sounded like her mom had been killed, but she didn't know for sure. She was supposed to say the mother was staying in Paris. Macy shook her head. Whatever had happened to Heather, it couldn't have been good.

Unless she and her mom really had stayed in Paris. It stood to reason that they would have wanted to get away from Chester. Maybe they were living it up under the Eiffel Tower—eating cold pie for breakfast—while Macy was forced to be the fill-in daughter.

She climbed into bed and pulled the covers up. She looked around the room before lying down. If she wasn't able to make her escape soon, she would go through the room to figure out what she could. She turned off the light on the nightstand.

As her head hit the pillow, she fell right to sleep. She dreamed of her family and Zoey. In her dreams, she was back home and everything was back to normal, except for everyone asking her where she had gone.

Macy sat up in bed, clutching the blankets. She didn't know what had woken her. She couldn't remember any bad dreams, nor did she think she heard any sounds. The house was quiet, so much so that she could hear some of the animals from the barn. Maybe that was what had woken her.

She certainly wasn't used to those noises when she slept in a bed.

The sun was starting to come up.

Could this be her chance? She climbed out of bed, holding her breath, fearful to make even a small noise. She tip-toed to the door, cringing each time her foot found a squeaky board.

Macy took a slow, quiet, deep breath before grabbing the doorknob. Should she get dressed first? In case she was able to make a run for it? She shook her head, holding her breath. She needed to check everything out first.

Turning the knob as slow as possible, she was relieved to find that it made no noise. She pulled the door open, silent except the noise of it sliding over the carpet. She stepped out of the room and gasped, covering her mouth.

Leaning against the wall, on the floor in front of her was the picture he had stolen from her house. Her parents, her brother and herself all smiled from the frame. She stared at it for a moment before closing the door as quietly as she could, her heart pounding nearly out of her chest.

She leaned against the closed door, trying to catch her breath.

He was reminding her of his threat to kill her family if she tried to get away. He was letting her know that he had gotten into her house once, and he could do it again.

Her heart sank. She couldn't risk the lives of her family.

What if she ran away, and then he went straight to her home and killed them?

She looked around the room. What if Chester had killed Heather and her mother? Someone crazy enough to kidnap would be nuts enough to kill.

Shaking, she climbed back into the warm bed. Even with the covers pulled up, she couldn't stop shivering.

What was she going to do? She couldn't live here, pretending to be Heather. Someone would have to figure it out, wouldn't they? He had said something about grandparents. Surely they would know Macy wasn't their granddaughter. They would have to. Even if Macy looked exactly like her, there was no way she spoke and acted like her.

Heather had to have gone to school and had friends. *They* would know she wasn't Heather. Zoey would know right away if someone posed as Macy.

Pulling her knees to her chest, Macy held her legs close, and took deep breaths. She couldn't stop shaking, nor would her heart slow down.

Even though she had called Chester "dad," he didn't trust her yet. How long would that take? When would she have enough trust to be able to sneak away?

She sighed and looked around the room, which was slowly getting lighter. If she stayed up a little longer, she'd have enough light to go through the room and see if she could find anything out about the girl who had lived there.

Hopefully, Heather was in Paris with her mom, but what were the chances of that? Who was Macy kidding? She couldn't imagine Chester leaving without them. He would have insisted they come with him, even if he had to threaten them. Either they had run away, like Macy wanted to, or Chester had done something to them, like he had threatened to do to her family.

She had finally stopped shaking. Even though she knew she would have to get up soon, she still felt sleepy. With a little more rest, she would have the energy to get away if given the chance.

Sometime later a loud, obnoxious beeping woke her up. She sat up, looking for the alarm, not remembering where it was. When she saw it, she hit every button until it turned off.

She would have to fix that before she set it again. Macy was a light sleeper. She didn't need an alarm loud enough to wake the dead.

Pulling the covers up, she wanted to stay in bed. She remembered the horrible room under the barn. At least this was better than that. She had an actual bed, and even food. She could even pee in a toilet. Who would have thought that would be a blessing?

Macy got up and went to the drawers, finding something to wear. The clothes were dull compared to what she normally wore, but at least they were clean.

She found a couple pieces of makeup in a box on top of the dresser—mascara and pale lip-gloss. She was going to have to get used to seeing herself without eyeliner, unless she was allowed to go to the store and get some—which she figured was out of the question.

Using the mirror on top of the dresser, she put the makeup on, refusing to think of how gross it was to wear someone else's products. Her mom had always lectured her on how unhygienic that was. But what else was she supposed to do? She was even wearing Heather's underwear, which she didn't want to think about.

When Macy was done, she looked in vain for a brush. She would have to go to the bathroom.

Macy took a deep breath. She didn't want to face the picture again. But when she opened the door, she was surprised to see it was gone.

Was he messing with her? She almost laughed at herself. Of course he was messing with her. That's what all of this was about.

She found a brush in the bathroom. Her hair had gone wild, sticking out in every direction. Brushing only made it worse. She dug through the drawers, hoping to find something. There were no gels or anything. Didn't the girl even have a cheap, drugstore brand flat iron? Something?

All she found was a small container full of hair bands. She pulled out a black one and pulled her hair back into a ponytail. Yuck. She hated how she looked in those. She saw some clips and pulled her bangs back too.

There was no way she would be able to style her side bangs without a flat iron or hairspray.

Macy looked in the mirror. She looked like someone else with her hair pulled back and barely any makeup. Was that the point? So she would forget who she really was?

Her stomach rumbled, so she went to the kitchen. Chester sat at the table, reading a newspaper. Some music played in the background. Music? *That's classy*, Macy thought sarcastically.

He looked up. "Oh, good. You have barely enough time to eat. I left the pie in the fridge, so it will be as cold as possible—just how you like it, Heather. Grab some and sit down. I've already eaten."

She nodded, not wanting to engage him in conversation. As she walked to the fridge, she could feel his eyes on her. She remembered him shoving her into the side of the truck, threatening her. Chills ran down her back, but she got the pie out, doing her best to act normal—whatever "normal" meant.

Macy opened a couple of cupboards, looking for a plate.

"Don't tell me you forgot where those are too, Heather. Over the microwave." He sighed with heavy dramatic flair. What a tool.

She grabbed a plate and put a piece of pie on it. She found the utensils on her first try. Then she sat down across from him, as far away as she could get. She ate the pie, which was too sweet for breakfast, trying to ignore him.

"You're not talkative, are you?"

Shoving pie into her mouth, she shrugged, not looking up at him.

"Well, I'm sure that will change in time. You have to get used to being here. So how did you sleep?"

She shrugged again.

"That's not an answer. How did you sleep?"

"Fine."

"Do you want to know what we're doing today?"

"Sure." Macy kept eating, not taking her eyes off the food.

"First, we're going to get your hair done."

She looked up at him in surprise. What did that mean?

"You look too different from how you did before our trip to France.

We'll need to lighten your hair. Your mom always insisted on getting your hair colored. Obviously all that's grown out. Then you'll look exactly like your old self. When we're done with that, your grandparents should be back. Won't that be fun? They've really missed you."

Macy's heart raced, and tears sprung to her eyes. She blinked them away.

"Don't look so crestfallen, Heather. Change is good. I think we'll cut your hair as well. We'll say you decided to do that while we were away. It was the style over there."

Her stomach twisted in knots. She didn't want to cut her hair—or color it. She liked it long and dark brown. Was he going to strip away everything about her identity? She remembered the pictures of Heather. She had long hair in every one of them. "But H—my hair was never short. Look at all the pictures over there."

"Like I said, change is good."

"Are you afraid I'm going to look too much like the pictures in the news with my hair long?" Macy hadn't meant to say that. She backed up, afraid of the look on his face.

"What did you say?"

"Um, that I'd like to talk about this?"

He leapt up and came at her, grabbing her arms and squeezing hard before forcing her out of her chair. "Don't ever talk back to me. Do you understand? Ever. Unless you want to find yourself back in the barn. Is that what you want?" He pushed her, shoving her against the fridge.

Macy shook her head.

"Good. Because your grandparents are coming soon, and you need to be on your best behavior. Not acting like this." He pulled her back and threw her against a cabinet, a handle jamming into her side.

Macy let out a cry.

He glared at her, his nostrils flaring. "Don't you forget it." He stormed out of the room.

Desperate

CHAD CHECKED HIS blog for comments, holding on to hope that someone would have seen Macy. Per the norm for the last few days, he hadn't been able to sleep. Even when he did manage to drift off, a nightmare would wake him up.

He always went to where he was loved—his blog. After the candlelight vigil in the park, he had written a heart-wrenching post about Macy's disappearance. He knew the news was national, and he was already getting some comments on his other posts asking about the situation, so a post about her was exactly what was needed.

It had helped him to feel better. Not only was he able to get his feelings, his own story, out there, but it might help to get her back too. His daughter could be anywhere, and his readers were from all over the world. He had hits from nearly every country on the globe.

Chad had uploaded all kinds of pictures of Macy onto the post. First, he had put their latest family photo. That was already on his "About Me" page. It was a perfect picture. Then he grabbed some from his phone and also Macy's social media accounts. Did all teenagers post so many pictures of themselves?

She had pictures of herself doing everything under the sun. He had griped about it before, but now, with her being gone, he couldn't have been more grateful. Not only could he use them on his blog, but they had become special to him in a way they never were before. He couldn't stop looking at them.

His heart broke, wishing he had taken more time for her. He had spent entirely too much time harping on her. He had told her to wear more colors, smile more, study more, eat some meat once in a while, and stop posting silly stuff all the time.

Why hadn't he taken some time to get to know her, instead of always trying to change her? Looking through the pictures now, he noticed how beautiful she was. She also looked a little sad, even through all the goofiness.

Hadn't he learned anything when he lost his parents in that car accident? He knew how suddenly someone he loved could be snatched from him.

Scrolling through the pictures on his post, he sighed. What if she had run away with that dipstick kid she met online? Would she come back, or had he pushed her so far away that she never wanted to return? Or what if the police were right and that kid wasn't a kid at all, but a child abductor?

Chad needed a new post. He needed to keep getting the word out about Macy. He went into his dashboard to schedule a new post for the next day when he noticed his stats. His blog had more than tripled its usual page views. In fact, it was close to quadruple.

People really *were* paying attention to his story about Macy. He needed to post about her often. The more he posted, the more likely it was that someone would recognize his daughter from somewhere. Maybe his blog would be what saved her.

He opened a new tab and went to Macy's profile again. There were hundreds of new messages posted from her friends. Chad saw that some of the kids had even put pictures of Macy along with their posts. He needed to put some of those in his upcoming blog posts.

After uploading about a dozen new pictures to the post, he realized he was out of words. What was there to say? There were no new developments in the case. She was still missing, and he wanted someone to find her. Chad couldn't handle her being gone any longer. Someone somewhere knew something, and his blog was the best way to reach that person.

Sure, the news was reaching a lot of people, but they weren't saying what he wanted them to say. Both times his family had been interviewed, what they said was edited down to practically nothing. At least on his blog, which ten thousand people were looking at every day now, he could say what he wanted.

People were so curious, and he was sure that the names of his entire family were being searched at unprecedented numbers. That was obviously why his blog was getting so many more hits than normal. He had to take advantage of that. He began typing again.

Thank you all for your concern about my daughter, Macy Mercer. This is obviously a sports blog, but you surely understand the posts about the horrors my family is enduring.

Writing about sports with my typical humor isn't in my heart, and I appreciate your understanding. To my fans, I'll get back into it as soon as I can—when Macy is back home, safe and sound. For those of you who are here to learn more about Macy, please see my last post. You'll find pictures not shown on the news sites, and you'll hear about everything from my own perspective, minus the media edits and BS.

Not that I don't appreciate the media getting the word out there, but if you know me, and I know many of you don't, I get tired of the media's crap on a regular basis. They only tell people what they want to hear. It's not real reporting.

My previous post, that's the real story. That's what's going on with my daughter. She snuck out to meet some boy online and now she's gone. All you girls reading this—learn from Macy's mistake. Don't meet a boy you don't know by yourself. If you feel the need to sneak out because you think your parents are too strict, then set up a group date. Please. Just stay safe.

Practically nothing is known about the guy that my daughter met online. His name was supposedly Jared, but all of his social profiles have been removed. The police think he might have actually been a man posing as a boy. It would have been easy for him to snatch a picture of some random kid and pretend to be a friendly teenager.

I hope to God that's not the case. I would much rather Macy be off with some harmless kid, sticking her tongue out at me for being overprotective. But with each passing hour, that scenario becomes less and less believable.

Seeing the worry in Macy's best friend's eyes tells me that my daughter hasn't contacted her either. If this were about Macy sneaking out or even running away to get our attention, she would have contacted her best friend. What fifteen-year-old girl could go that long without instant messaging, or whatever it is kids are up to this month?

Please, please pay attention to the pictures in this post and my last one. There are pictures of her with her hair pulled back, down straight, curled, and wearing hats. Who knows what she could look like when she walks down the street next to you?

Macy didn't take any extra clothes or makeup. She wasn't planning on being gone for more than the evening. Someone has my baby girl, and one of you could be the one to help find her. Thank you again.

Chad pushed the schedule button and then sat back in his chair. So much for not having any words. He took a deep breath, ignoring the lump in his throat. What else could he do? His work had given him the week off with pay, so he had nothing to do except worry about Macy.

He looked at his scheduled post, scanning for errors. He couldn't see any mistakes, but that didn't mean anything. He wasn't thinking straight.

Going back to Macy's Facebook profile, he saw even more comments from friends. Or at least he assumed they were her friends. Maybe she had opened her page up for anyone to see. It had obviously been too long since he had given her a lecture about Internet safety. He was online all the time, he should have been more aware of what his kids were doing.

Reading all the messages, his eyes became heavy. He looked out the window and saw that it was still dark. He knew he wouldn't sleep long anyway, so he turned off his screen and went to the couch at the far end of his office. He pulled an afghan over himself and fell right to sleep.

Changes

MACY STOOD BY the window in Heather's room, looking outside. Absentmindedly, she ran her fingers along the tops of the nails that kept her inside. Leaves lay all over the ground, and the ones in the shade still had frost on them.

She heard a noise behind her and turned around. Chester held a gray plastic bag in one hand. "We have something to take care of."

"What?" Macy eyed the bag, unable to tell what was inside.

"No questions. Follow me."

Her shoulders slumped, and she followed him into the bathroom.

"Ladies first." He moved aside.

Macy's heart pounded as she stepped inside. He grabbed a dark green towel and wrapped it around her shoulders. Then he pulled a white box from the plastic bag and set it on the counter. It was a box of hair dye.

"What's that?" Macy exclaimed. He was actually going to change her hair color, wasn't he?

"I said no questions." He opened the box, looked at the instructions, poured one bottle of stuff into another, and then shook it. The liquid turned a bright, orange color. He turned to her, and Macy held her breath. He had to be joking.

Chester squeezed the cold liquid onto her hair and rubbed it in. He piled the hair in a messy heap on her head and told her not to move. Then he pulled out his phone and appeared to play a game.

Macy looked into the mirror in horror. What was he doing to her hair? After what felt like an eternity, he forced her head into the sink and rinsed out the dye. She gasped in shock at the sight of her newly colored hair.

"Use the towel to dry it." He shoved another towel at her.

She stared at him in disbelief.

"Was I speaking in a foreign language? Dry your hair!"

Macy flipped her head down in front of her stomach and dried it as best she could with only a towel.

Chester pointed to the toilet. "Sit."

Blood drained from Macy's head. "You want me to go to the bathroom?"

His eyebrows came together. "No. I'm cutting your hair. Now sit!"

She sat.

Chester pulled out a large pair of scissors.

"Have you cut hair before?"

"I watched a video online. Now shut up."

Macy's stomach twisted in knots. She closed her eyes, unable to watch. The slicing, snipping sounds of the scissors sounded all around her head.

"Done," Chester said. "Now, we need to get ready for your grandparents' return. They're eager to see you. Do you remember what to say when they ask about your mom?"

Macy clenched her fists. "She's still in Paris."

"Perfect. After lunch, it'll be time to clean."

Macy nodded and stood up. She glanced at the mirror, almost unable to recognize herself. It was still her face, but she looked so different with lighter, shorter hair. To her surprise, the haircut actually looked almost professional.

Chester directed her to the kitchen to make sandwiches. He turned on the TV and flipped through the channels, landing on the news. The newscasters were discussing a missing person. Then her latest school photo flashed on the screen.

Macy's heart skipped a beat, and then it raced.

He changed the station to some western movie. He turned to her as though nothing had happened. "Put plenty of meat on my sandwich."

She nodded, and went to the fridge to see what she could put on the sandwiches. Shaking, she pulled out all vegetables for hers. Once those were on the counter, she found stuff he wanted: lunch meats, mayo, and cheese. She didn't see any vegan mayo, so she'd have to use the one made with egg.

If she could even eat. She was still shaking from the shock of seeing her face—and old hairstyle—on the news. Did that mean her family knew she hadn't really run away? Or were they treating her case as a missing runaway? She'd barely heard anything before Chester changed the station.

Macy took a deep breath, trying to calm herself. She was going to spill something if she didn't. She spread the four pieces of bread on the counter and organized everything else. Once her hands were steady, she made his sandwich. Then she cut the cucumbers and everything else she needed for hers.

She put the food away, and then put the sandwiches on plates. She took them to the table before grabbing some grapes and chips, setting those in the middle of the table. Hopefully that would meet his expectations.

She sat down, hoping he wouldn't notice. But he did. He got up and sat next to her. "This looks great. You always make a great lunch, Heather."

Macy shrugged, not looking up. She bit into her sandwich, trying to ignore the strong taste of non-vegan mayo. It assaulted her taste buds, but she knew that was the least of her problems.

Her family was actually looking for her, but they had no idea where she was. *She* didn't even know.

Chester stood up. "When you're done, it'll be time to clean up. You can clean the kitchen and living room. I'm going to go back and clean the bathroom and your grandparents' room."

Was he actually going to leave her alone?

Macy waited, expecting him to return or something else to happen. There was no way that he would leave her in the big, open front part of the house…was there? Unless it was some kind of test to see if she would listen. She looked around for a hidden camera, but couldn't see anything.

Her heart started racing. Was this her chance to get away, or would she end up back in the barn? He wouldn't do that, though. He was too eager for her to meet his parents.

She tip-toed into the hallway leading to the front door. He was down the other hall, near the bedrooms.

"Did you need something?" he asked.

"No. I was looking for something, but I…don't see it." She hurried back into the living room. Going through the front door wasn't going to work. If she went that way again and he was still there testing her, he would definitely know something was up.

Macy wandered around the living room, looking at the pictures again. His parents looked like nice, happy people, but they had raised him, so who knew? They could be monsters, too. She looked at another picture of Heather. It was unnerving, because the picture could have been Macy—especially with the new haircut and color.

The house was still quiet. She looked around at the big windows. If she was able to open one and get outside, she should be able to get enough of a head start to get away. It didn't matter that she had no idea where she was. She could figure it out when she found a road.

Holding her breath, she looked around. She couldn't see anything stopping her. The windows weren't locked down. This was her chance, and she had to take it right then. Who knew when she would be able to try to get away again?

She walked over to one of the windows. Her pulse was on fire as she looked for a way to unlock the window. It was unlike any window she had ever seen. There were ropes at the top, which were obviously used for opening and closing it somehow. She would have to open it and hope for the best. The window only needed to be opened enough for her to squeeze out.

Macy saw a knob and twisted it around. Something clicked. She turned around to make sure that he hadn't returned. She was still alone. She put her fingers in two grooves at the bottom and pulled up. The window opened!

She pulled it further, but not much because it was surprisingly heavy. That's when a loud, high-pitched screaming sound surrounded her.

The alarm.

He came around the hallway, glaring at her. The look on his face was scarier than it had been at any other point. Macy backed up and looked at the window, which still wasn't open wide enough for her to squeeze through.

"I...I was just—"

Eyes narrowed, he grabbed her elbow, squeezing painfully. He dragged her to the front door where a coat rack stood. He pushed it aside and punched buttons on a white box. The alarm finally stopped.

"The alarm is set. If any of the doors or windows are opened, that horrible alarm you hate so much will go off. It looks like you figured that out already, didn't you?" He squeezed harder, his eyebrows coming together.

He grabbed her other arm and shook her so that her head hit one of the hooks on the coat rack. He shoved her back, digging her back into the wooden rack. Jackets pushed around her face. "I thought we had an understanding. You were going to obey. We need to get the house cleaned before your grandparents get here, Heather." He yanked her back and threw her against the opposite wall.

She hit her head again. "I thought we could use some fresh air. Look at the window. It's only opened a crack."

He grabbed her shoulders and pushed her further against the wall and lifted her so that she wasn't able to touch the floor. "No fresh air! We're already out in the country. We couldn't ask for better quality air. Don't do anything to change the house—ever again! Do you understand me?" Spit flew onto her face. Macy couldn't wipe it away.

She nodded.

His angry eyes came closer to hers. "It looks as though I'm going to have to do the cleaning myself. You're going to spend some time in your room and think about what you've done. When your grandparents get here, you need to be on your best behavior. Do you understand?"

"Yes." She squirmed, hoping he would let go of her.

"When they get here, you're not to try anything funny. Nothing! The only reason I'm not sending you back to the barn is because they're so close to arriving. Keep that in mind." He shoved her and then let go.

Macy fell to the ground and then stood up. At least she had tried to get away. It hadn't worked, but she had tried.

Discovery

THE BEDROOM DOOR closed behind Macy. She could hear something slide against it, keeping her inside. She sighed, looking around the room.

She needed to calm down. Obviously, there was no texting or online games, but maybe Heather had some books. Then Macy could at least escape into her mind for a little while.

She couldn't see any books, but there had to be something. Macy would even take classic literature at that point, as much as she would have preferred to read about some hot vampires or werewolves.

Where would books be? Maybe near the stuffed animals. Macy had all but ignored that part of the room. There was a small shelf underneath the little hammock holding the toys. She sat down and looked at it. The top row was full of DVDs, which she wouldn't be able to watch.

Macy scanned the books on the next shelf. Most of them *were* literary—things teachers forced kids to read. One had an interesting title that she had never heard of. She grabbed it and noticed that it felt odd.

What was that? She narrowed her eyes and looked inside the book. It didn't open as easily as a book should. When she had it open, she saw that it had been hollowed out and another book rested in it. It looked like a diary.

Her heart stopped. Was that Heather's journal?

This might be her opportunity to find out more about what happened.

Her pulse pounded so loud in her ears that she was afraid Chester would hear it. She took a couple of deep, long breaths. She had to focus. Once she calmed down, she turned to the first entry. Her hands shook.

The first entries were pretty basic stuff.

Heather liked some boy at school, she hated homework, one girl in the neighborhood wouldn't stop bothering her…wait. Neighborhood? Where had they been living? Definitely not on the farm. There was nothing even close to neighbors. Not once had Macy been able to see anything other than farmland.

She wanted to read every word in the journal, but knew she didn't have much time left. She flipped through the pages, skimming the first few lines of each entry.

One caught her attention about a third of the way through. *My mom is still not back.* Macy stopped. She had never bought the story about Heather's mom running off with some guy in France—not that Macy would blame her for running from Chester.

Macy went back to the previous entry and read it word for word. More about the boy that Heather adored. Heather wasn't sure if the boy even knew she was alive, but she couldn't stop thinking about him. It was getting in the way of her schoolwork, and her dad could tell something was up. She wasn't going to admit to him that she was distracted by a boy. He would freak out.

No kidding.

She read on. Heather went on about the boy's eyes and some answer he gave in a class. Then Macy held her breath. His name was Jared. Heather had been in love with a boy named Jared. Chills ran down her spine. That couldn't be a coincidence. Obviously, that was why Chester had chosen that name. She looked back at the paper.

> *This morning when I got up, Dad was eating breakfast alone. That was really strange, because Mom and Dad pretty much—like always—eat together. Then I joined them for a few minutes since they make me have breakfast every day. I'm like the only kid in school who eats breakfast. Everyone else sleeps in as long as possible and then eats cold pastries or something. Anyway, I have no idea why I'm going on about that. Guess this is my place to ramble.*
>
> *So I asked Dad where she was, and he wouldn't look me in the eyes. That was weird, but I was worried that she was sick or something, so I didn't really think much about it. He just said she wasn't*

there. Obviously, I could see that. So I kept asking questions, and he finally looked at me.

The look in his eyes was scary. I'd never seen anything like it. I wanted to run out of the house. He said she had some stuff to take care of. Of course I wanted to know what kind of stuff, but he wouldn't say. I wanted to know when she'd be back, but he wouldn't tell me that either. He said don't worry about it. Don't worry? How was I supposed to do that?

He told me to sit down and eat. I didn't feel like eating at all, but you know how he gets. I made a small bowl of oatmeal. I didn't think I could keep any more down. I knew I'd probably piss him off, but I kept asking questions about Mom. He wouldn't tell me anything. Finally, he slammed a fist on the table and told me to go to school.

Since I knew I wouldn't get anything else out of him, I got up and left. I hope she's okay. It's so weird that she hasn't gotten a hold of me. I mean, she could text me or send me an email. Usually, she sends me goofy texts in the middle of the day. She says she wanted to make sure I smiled at least once at school.

There hasn't been anything new on her profile either. She always posts articles that she finds interesting. By always, I mean lots every day. The last was last night. Almost a full day ago. Her friends are even posting, asking if she's okay. Wish I could answer for her and say something, but Dad won't get off his laptop and give me any answers.

Guess that means I gotta get my homework done now or I'm going to have more late assignments. I'm close to a few teachers contacting my parents about that. I keep hoping Mom will come through the door. Doesn't she know I would worry? Why would she leave without saying anything?

Macy read on, skimming over the next few entries. Mostly, it was Heather pouring out her worries about her mom. She wanted to know if Heather ever found out. Macy wanted to know if Chester had killed her mom.

A few pages later, an entry started with *My mom is back.* Macy held her breath and continued reading.

When I got home from school today, Mom was sitting on our couch. She didn't even look up when I came into the room. I stood right in front of her, but she was staring off to the side. She was holding on to the blanket so tight her hands were turning white.

I kept saying 'Mom' over and over, but it was like she couldn't hear me. I started crying and begged her to look at me. Finally, she turned, but it felt like she was looking through me. I finally sat down and leaned my head against her. I was crying, but she didn't even notice. She never ignores me when I'm upset. Never!

What had happened to her? Where had she been?

We sat there not talking for so long, I finally stopped crying. There was nothing left in me. I started asking her questions about where she had been and stuff, but she kept acting like she wasn't even there. She wouldn't say a thing! Not one thing. I asked the same questions over and over. I hoped that maybe she would finally answer one of them.

I know I sound like a baby, but I want my Mommy back. I missed her so much when she was gone. It was so hard not talking with her. Some kids hate talking with their parents, but not me. My mom is my best friend. I can tell her anything—anything at all. She doesn't judge me about anything, no matter what it is. Boys, kids doing drugs, you name it. Nothing's off limits with her. She doesn't go crazy like some of my friends' parents.

Even when I wanted a pink streak in my hair, she was behind me. Dad said no way, but Mom let me get one underneath so I could pull my hair up at school and all the kids could see it there, then I could take it down before Dad got back from work. She gets me. Not even my friends get me like she does. I can't even explain it.

Macy sat back, taking it in. It must have been nice for Heather to be able to talk to her mom about anything. The pink streak reminded Macy of Zoey—not that Zoey would ever want to wear anything pink, but Zoey always wanted to do things to stand out.

What had happened to Heather's mom? Macy had been certain that she had disappeared forever. It wouldn't have surprised her if she was dead. Would this diary tell her what happened to them?

She listened, not hearing anything. The last thing she wanted was to be caught reading the diary. Chester would take it away.

My mom wouldn't get up for dinner. She just sat on that couch staring at nothing. I didn't even know if she knew she was home. Why wouldn't she acknowledge me? Not even a nod of the head or something? Something!

I couldn't even look at Dad. I knew he had something to do with this. Who knows what? But something, and he wasn't talking. The stupid jerk was acting like everything was fine. He thought I should be happy that she was back. Of course I'm glad she's back, but I'm not even close to happy about how she's acting. How can he not be concerned?

After dinner, I got my homework and did it on the couch. I talked to Mom like everything was normal, even though it's totally not. It couldn't be more not-normal. I'm pissed off, but trying to put on a smile. I told her about my friends and the latest drama with the stupid cheerleaders who have been playing pranks on us. Then I talked about Jared and how I still couldn't bring myself to talk to him, and about Parker who likes me, but I really don't like him like that.

Dad overheard me talking about the boys and he got upset. He lives in the dark ages and thinks I shouldn't have any interest in boys. Never mind the fact that he had girlfriends when he was younger than me. For some reason, I'm supposed to be above that. Hypocrite. Sometimes I think Mom and I need to move across the country to get away from him.

I don't know if she'll ever get over what's going on though. I mean, I hate to think this, but what if she has brain damage? What if she's never going to be herself again? I can't think of anything else that would make her like this.

Macy read on. There were several more days' worth of entries where Heather essentially said the same things. Her mom wouldn't respond to anything. She wasn't sure if her mom was even eating, but she had to be getting up to go to the bathroom at some points, so Heather thought maybe she was eating, only not in front of her.

Then about four days later, something changed.

I slept in really late today. Usually, I sleep in on the weekends, but not like this. It was afternoon when I woke up. I guess I needed it after all the stress of worrying about Mom. Even with having her back, my stress is still through the roof. Maybe worse. Before, I could at least tell myself that it was possible she was on a personal vacation. I don't have that now.

Anyway, I got up and Mom was standing by the window. Standing! I didn't know if I should say anything or not. I was almost afraid that if I said something, she'd like go back to the couch and never leave again. So I went and stood by her. She didn't seem to notice.

I whispered to her and she looked at me. She actually looked at *me! Not through me. I had a million questions running through my head, but I asked her what she was looking at. It seemed like a safe question. I didn't want to send her back to hiding inside herself again. I decided not to ask where she had been, at least not yet.*

She pointed to a kid riding a bike across the street. Then she started talking about when I was little and learning to ride a bike. I didn't know what that had to do with anything, but I let her keep talking. She was actually talking. Would she keep talking until she told me where she had been and what caused her to act like this?

Mom talked about my childhood for a little while and then stopped. She looked outside for a while, even after the kid went inside. I asked her if she wanted to eat something, but she shook her head. At least that was a response. I wanted to ask her about where she went, but I was so scared that she wouldn't keep talking.

I didn't know what to do. I've never been so scared in my life. What if I said the wrong thing? I just wanted her back, the way she had been before. Finally, I took her hand. She actually smiled! Then she moved a little closer to me, but she still didn't say anything. I stood there with her until she wanted to take a nap. She went back to the couch. It's pretty much her new bed now.

Should I dare ask about where she went? I don't know what to do.

Macy continued reading about Heather's fears. She wrote them out over and over, most likely because she had been trying to figure out how she felt about what was going on. She hadn't told any of her friends, because she didn't want anyone thinking her mom was weird. So the diary had been her only confidant.

Heather didn't mention it, but Macy couldn't help wondering if she was also afraid of her dad. He would undoubtedly lose it if she told anyone at school what was going on with her mom.

The next day's entry showed that Heather had made a decision.

After getting all my worries out in here, I decided to ask Mom my questions when I woke up. I was so anxious about it, I woke up early. Dad was still sleeping, so I had that to my advantage.

Mom was back at the window again. That had to be a good sign, right? I walked right up to her, took her hand, and said good morning. She squeezed my hand and talked about the squirrels and birds playing in the yard. I waited for her to pause and then I prepared myself to ask my questions.

I was so nervous that I was holding my breath without even realizing it. So, I had to take a deep breath before saying anything. Then I asked her where she went. I told her that I had missed her a lot.

She squeezed my hand again and then looked into my eyes. My eyes! She asked if I wanted to sit. I would have agreed to anything at that point. So we sat on the couch and she covered both of us, not herself, with the afghan. She looked around. She was obviously nervous about something—probably Dad. I told her that he was sleeping. I waited a minute and then asked her again where she had been.

She looked at me and said, "The barn."

What barn? I asked her if she meant the one at Grandma and Grandpa's. She nodded yes.

Macy turned the page. It was the last one and nothing else was written.

"That can't be all," Macy whispered. "There has to be more." She carried the diary back to the shelf and looked behind all the books. There were no more diaries. She slid it back into place where she'd found it.

Macy lifted the mattress and dug through Heather's stuffed animals, not finding anything. She looked through the clothes in the dresser. There was no diary there either.

The doorknob jiggled and Macy went to the bed and sat, pretending to act natural.

Deeper

CHESTER WALKED INTO the bedroom. "Get out to the living room. Your grandparents are here."

Macy followed him out there and looked out the window. The old car pulled up the long driveway at a snail's pace. What were Chester's parents like? And how was she ever going to convince them she was their granddaughter? They were bound to figure it out. And what would Chester do?

The rocks in the driveway crunched as the car came closer to the house. Macy put the picture back into place and looked out the window again. The car doors opened, and two people about her own grandparents' age got out of the car. The lady had big glasses and short, curly hair. It was probably supposed to be black, but it shone blue in the sun. The guy was mostly bald, except for a thin line of grayish-white hair along the back of his head.

A wave of fear ran through her, and her heart started racing. When was she going to get away? This couldn't actually be her new life. It couldn't be. She turned to look inside. The room felt as though it was going to swallow her up. Was it actually shrinking?

"Wipe that sour look off your face, Heather," Chester said. "You need to greet your grandparents with a smile." His gaze bore into her soul. Macy could almost feel the evil emanating from him. He narrowed his eyes. "I need to see you smile. Smile, dammit!"

Her throat closed up, while at the same time tears filled her eyes.

His lips turned white as they formed a straight line. Anger covered his face. "Don't make this difficult, Heather. You don't want to go back into the barn, do you?"

The blood drained from her face. She shook her head. "No, please. Don't."

"Then smile." The lines around his eyes deepened as he furrowed his eyebrows. "If you like that bed more than you like bales of hay, you better get over yourself and show your grandparents how happy you are to see them. Do I make myself clear?"

Out of the corner of her eye, she could see them walking toward the house. She swallowed, and then nodded. She forced a smile.

He stepped closer to her. "That's pathetic. You couldn't convince a blind person you were happy."

A tear spilled onto her face and then forced her smile even wider.

He frowned, shaking his head. Stepping closer, he grabbed her shirt. Macy gasped, stepping back. He tightened his grip and pulled her forward. She could smell him, he was so close. "You need to stop being a spoiled brat and get over yourself. Do I make myself clear? Do I?" Spit sprayed onto her face.

Macy nodded, blinking back tears.

"Stop being selfish and make your grandparents feel welcome. They haven't seen you in a long time. Pull yourself together." He shoved her backwards. The window sill jabbed her in the back.

Without thinking, she reached back to rub the spot.

"You're not going to make this difficult on me, are you?"

She shook her head.

"Good. Because if you do, I guarantee you'll regret it." The look on his face told Macy that he meant it.

"Okay." She already regretted ever getting into the truck with him. The last thing she needed was to regret anything else. She took a deep breath. All she needed to was to get through this, and then she would find a way out. Even if she had to run out the front door, sounding the alarm in the middle of the night. That would give her enough of a head start that she could get away.

She had already had some meals and her strength had gotten a lot better. She wasn't back to normal, but she wasn't as weak as she had been earlier, in that dungeon—and there was no way she was going back there.

He got in her face, so close that he bumped her nose with his. "Remember, if you keep acting like an ungrateful brat, you're going to wish you had never been born. Make your grandparents feel like the most important people alive." He stood back, adjusted his shirt, and then walked toward the front door. He reached for the alarm system. Macy could hear him pushing the buttons. He turned back to her. "I'm going to reset it so that if any door or window is opened, everyone in the house will be alerted, so don't get any ideas."

Staring at him, she refused to acknowledge his words. She was going to hang onto whatever shreds of dignity she could, even if it was something as small as that.

As she heard the alarm disengage, a key sounded in the front door.

Chester turned around and glared at her. The look in his eyes told Macy that he would hurt her if he had to. Maybe even kill her. She had never had someone look at her like that before. Cold fear shot through her.

Still giving her that look, he pointed to the ground near him, the intensity of the anger and hate burning deeper on his face. "Get over here. Now."

Macy ran over to him. She would rather do what he said than find out what he would do if she didn't.

The door opened. He turned his attention to his parents. "Mom, Dad. It's so good to see you." He smiled as though he hadn't just threatened Macy. "Let me help you with your bags." He stepped forward, taking both of their suitcases. "Did you have a nice trip?"

Macy stared, unable to pay attention to what they were saying. Before she knew it, she was wrapped in an embrace. Her *grandma* was giving her a hug. Macy knew she had to play the part well if she wanted to keep Chester happy. She put her arms around the old lady, hugging her tight.

"It's so good to see you, Heather." The woman stepped back, looking Macy over. "You're so beautiful—and you haven't changed a bit. Except that you're taller. My, how you've grown. Look at her, George."

The elderly man turned to her and smiled. "She looks exactly like you when we met, Ingrid."

Ingrid looked back at Macy. "You know, you're right. We could have been twins had we been the same age. There's no doubt we're related, is there?" She gave Macy a warm smile.

Macy nodded, not sure how to respond to that.

George looked at her. "Where's your mom, Heather?"

"I...." Macy's eyes widened. What was the story? Had she been told what she was supposed to say about her fake mom? If she had been, she couldn't remember. Everything was a blur, and really, she didn't care about some fake story.

Her captor glared at her again. He then turned to his parents, giving them a fake-genuine look of sadness. Macy knew better. "I didn't want to tell you over the phone, but she decided to stay in Paris."

"What? Why?" Concern washed over Ingrid's face.

"Let's sit down and talk about this over lunch," said George.

Ingrid shook her head. "I need to hear this first."

"We can hear it while we get lunch ready." He shook his head, and then walked around them to the kitchen.

Everyone followed him into the kitchen, where he was already pulling everything out of the fridge. Ingrid joined him, throwing things into a large pot. Was she going to make soup from scratch? Macy watched her in awe, forgetting that she was being held against her will. She had always wanted to learn to cook, to really cook—from scratch, but her mom never wanted to make anything. Why make it when you could buy it?

Ingrid looked at Macy. "Come help me, Heather."

"Okay." Despite everything, Macy actually smiled. At least she was going to get *something* out of this nightmare. Maybe she could cook her family some real food from scratch when she got back. Ingrid handed her an apron, and then pointed to some potatoes.

"Peel those."

Macy nodded, slipping the apron over her head. She wanted to kick herself for feeling excitement, but it wasn't as though the sweet, old lady had anything to do with her kidnapping. Macy grabbed the peeler and rubbed it against the potato. Not even a thin slice of skin came off.

"Oh! Has it been that long?" Ingrid exclaimed. She grabbed the potato from Macy, glaring back at her captor. "Haven't you had her make any food all this time? Don't tell me you've been buying her packaged food, Chester."

He glared at his mom. "You know I go by Chet."

She shook her head. "Not around here, you don't, Chester."

A smile spread across Macy's face. Chester shot her a menacing look, but it didn't have the same effect with his parents between them.

Ingrid brought the potato out from the sink. "First things first, Heather. Now that it's washed, you hold it at an angle like this. Watch." She slid the peeler down, and as she did, a perfect slice of potato skin fell onto the cutting board. "Now you do it."

Macy gave it a try, and before long, she had a perfectly peeled potato. She was actually proud of herself. She managed to chop it into small pieces without cutting herself in the process, though there were a few close calls.

Soon, she and Ingrid had put together a full pot of soup. Ingrid winked at her. "That will be ready in time for dinner. Shall we eat the sandwiches your grandpa made?"

Macy was disappointed she would have to wait so long for the soup, but at the same time, she wasn't really all that hungry. Sandwiches would be perfect. They all sat at the table. As Macy stared at the couldn't-be-less-vegan sandwich, she decided that given everything she had been through, she was going to stop thinking about her veganism. She needed strength, and that could only come from eating. She could go back to being a vegan once she was back home.

Maybe after this whole ordeal, her parents would even support her food lifestyle. That was another benefit to the nightmare. She bit into the roast beef sandwich with five layers of cheese, unsuccessfully pretending it was avocados and cucumbers with sesame seeds. It definitely wasn't that.

Ingrid finished hers before Macy got through her first half. She looked at her son. "All right, Chester. What happened with Karla? Why is she still in France?"

He glared at his mom. "Chet, Mom. Call me, Chet."

"Where's Karla?"

"In France, Mother." He slammed down his sandwich.

George glared at him. "Don't treat our table that way, son. What's going on with your wife?"

Chester made a face. "She doesn't want to be part of our family anymore. I didn't want to talk about it in front of Heather. You know how close they were."

Ingrid dropped her fork. "She doesn't want…? I don't understand. You and Heather are her life. I've never seen a more doting mother."

"Until she met Jacques, Mom."

Ingrid's mouth dropped open. "Chester, you don't mean to tell me she met someone else?"

"Chet! My name is Chet." He glared at Macy, who was again, trying not to smile.

"Fine." Ingrid stared at him. "What did Jacques have that you don't?"

"Do we need to talk about this? Heather doesn't need to hear about it."

George looked at him. "It does no good to hide the truth from anyone, son. Tell us what happened."

He sighed. "Karla fell in love with the city. She wanted to move there, but I didn't. We fought a lot, and she started going out for day trips on her own. That's when she met him. He promised her the world. She came back one day, demanding that we move there or she would leave us for him. I told her no, it was time to come home. But she said she was staying there. I tried to reason with her, but she wouldn't listen. You can't use logic with crazy. So she gave up her family for the lights of the city. Are you happy now? She ruined our lives, and now you know everything."

"That's awful. My poor baby." Ingrid got up, walked around the table, and wrapped her son in a hug.

Macy watched his face. He looked as though he really, truly believed his lies. She was almost convinced herself.

Room

As much as Macy hated her new bedroom, it was better than spending any time with Chester.

Never before had she hated someone so much. He was such a horrible person. Even his own parents got irritated with him. He argued with them, often even ordering them around. They weren't rude to him, but she wouldn't have blamed them if they had been. If she ever had a kid who talked to her like that, she wouldn't take it.

Their early morning conversation drifted into the bedroom, and she could smell coffee brewing. They were probably getting breakfast ready. At least they didn't appear to expect her. She went to the bathroom, trying to be as quiet as possible.

When she finished she almost flushed out of habit, but then decided against it. If she did that, she may as well have rang a bell and shouted that she was awake.

Not wanting to wash her hands for the same reasons, she squirted some sanitizer onto her hands.

Macy tip-toed back to the room, praying she wouldn't be caught. Even just a few more minutes of solitude would be appreciated. She made it back to the bedroom and closed the door. What a relief.

Before she could even crawl back into bed, she heard the doorknob turn behind her. She jumped up and ran to the dresser.

The door opened. "So you're up." Was his tone harsh, or was it her imagination?

She nodded, flipping through clothes.

"Look at me."

Her blood ran cold. She hadn't imagined the tone. What had she done to upset him this time? She swallowed and turned to face him.

"Were you up already?"

She stared at him. No matter what she said, it would probably be the wrong answer. What did he want to hear?

"I asked you a question." He narrowed his eyes and stepped closer.

Macy dropped the pants back into the drawer. It was probably better to tell him the truth. For whatever reason, he probably knew. She nodded.

He moved closer, looking angrier with each step.

Macy swallowed, looking around. Even if there was an exit, she would be stupid to try and avoid him. She would upset him further, and then probably end up in the barn again. Was he mad that she had gone back to the bedroom?

Chester stopped. He was only about an inch from her face. She could smell coffee and eggs. He grabbed her arms. "Don't ever walk away from the bathroom without flushing. Do you understand? That's gross. Gross! Do you know what kind of germs live in there?"

"I—I didn't know. At home, we don't flush if someone is sleeping. If it—"

He stepped even closer, bumping into her forehead with his. "*This* is your home. I don't care what happens in other houses, but here, we flush. Every time. I don't care if you're sick and barely conscious. You flush. Do you understand me?"

She nodded. "I didn't want to disturb any—"

"No excuses. Don't do it again. You've been warned." He narrowed his eyes further, deep creases around his eyes showed.

Macy's eyes widened. "Okay."

He continued to stare, still touching her face. How long was he going to stand there?

"I won't forget."

Mistake

MACY SIGHED AS the third rerun of *Night Court* began. It was actually a funny show, but she really wanted to get out of the living room. She needed to find a way to get out of the house.

Weren't old people supposed to go to bed early? She looked at the clock for the five-hundredth time. It was nine, and she had been watching reruns with Chester and her fake grandparents for hours. Their only break had been for dinner. The soup had been delicious, and Ingrid promised to teach her to make other kinds.

She looked around the room as canned laughter roared in the background. Chester was fidgeting. Obviously, he wasn't all that excited about the show either. Ingrid and George appeared to be having the time of their lives, laughing along with the TV every time someone said something funny.

Usually when Macy watched TV, she was busy texting or playing a game. Her family never just sat in front of the TV. Her dad usually had his laptop. He didn't want to take too long to respond to a comment on his blog. Her mom and brother texted as much as she did.

Her legs ached from sitting so long. She stood up.

Chester looked at her. "What are you doing?"

"Stretching my legs. I have to go to the bathroom."

He glared at her. "We're spending time with your grandparents."

"Let the girl use the bathroom," George said, without taking his attention off the show.

Macy went to the bathroom, finding it hard to believe that she was going into a bathroom because it was more exciting than the alternative. She needed a change of scenery and couldn't take anymore 80s fashion or hairstyles, much less the corny jokes.

She went to the bathroom and washed her hands three times. The last thing she wanted to do was to go out there and watch more TV. What she wouldn't give to be able to text. She stopped. Her phone couldn't be far. In fact, it was probably in Chester's room. He had said he used it to post on her profile, right?

Again, everything was a blur. It was hard to keep anything straight, but at any rate he had to have it. She opened the door as slow as possible and looked up and down the hall. No one was in there. She could hear a beer commercial coming from the living room.

Her heart pounded so loud she was sure the others could hear it. She knew they couldn't, so she did her best to ignore it. She went across the hall, holding her breath. She was listening for anyone coming, but couldn't hear much over her heart and the TV blaring. George spoke pretty loud; Macy thought he might be hard of hearing. Maybe that would be to her advantage, since no one would be able to hear her sneaking into Chester's room.

Even so, she would need to hurry. He would probably check on her if she took too long. Macy opened his door. It squeaked a little, but not loud enough for anyone else to hear.

The room was dark and chilly. He had to have kept the heat off completely to get it that cold. She got the chills as she stood, looking for where her phone might be. She scanned the room, letting her eyes adjust.

Macy was about to give up when she spotted her clothes in a corner, near a dresser and a chair. Hadn't she thrown them away? Why was he keeping them? They were disgusting. She looked back down the hall. Seeing no one, she walked toward the clothes she would never wear again. She rifled through them, not finding her phone.

There was a stack of papers on the dresser next to her clothes. She picked up the papers and saw her phone behind them. She picked it up, knowing it was too easy. The power button did nothing, which meant the battery was either dead or had been removed. She tried turning it on again, but of course it didn't work. It felt lighter than usual, so she was sure the battery had been taken out.

She opened a drawer full of socks and searched it, hoping to find her battery. It wasn't there. She closed the drawer, and then heard something. She froze. It was footsteps.

Someone was coming her way, and she had left the bedroom door open. Why hadn't she closed it? She looked around for a hiding spot, but Chester appeared in the doorway before Macy could move.

He looked around. At first, she thought he didn't see her, but then she realized his eyes were adjusting. She was about to duck to the ground when he stared in her direction. His eyes narrowed. "What are you doing in here?"

"I…uh, went into the wrong room." It sounded more like a question than a statement, and definitely sounded like a lie. Hopefully, he wouldn't notice.

Taking a few steps toward her, he kept staring at her. "Then why didn't you walk out once you realized your error?" He stared at the phone in her hand.

"I was bored. I wanted to play a game."

Anger flashed over his face. "Bored? You're worried about being bored?"

"I was just—"

"How could you even think that?" He took a few more steps closer. He was close enough to grab her if he wanted. "After spending all that time in the barn, I would think watching some funny shows with your grandparents, after a couple nice meals, might I add, would be a treat. But it's not enough for you?" He took another step.

She swallowed, taking a step back. "I usually play games or text when I watch TV. It's just—"

He grabbed her arm, squeezing hard. Macy tried to push him away, but he only added more pressure. "We're here to spend some time with your grandparents. They haven't seen you in over a year. Forget about games and texting. The only thing you need to worry about is spending time with them. Didn't you see how excited they were to see you?"

Macy didn't respond.

Chester twisted her arm, causing sharp pains.

She let out a cry of pain. "That hurts."

He furrowed his eyebrows. "Answer my question."

"What?" Her arm hurt so bad she couldn't even remember what he had asked.

"Your grandparents. Didn't you see how excited they were to see you?" He twisted her arm even further.

Macy winced. "Yes. Will you stop?"

He shoved her back, jamming her side into the dresser. "Stay out of my room. Got it? Don't ever come in here again."

She nodded, again trying to push his hand off her arm. He shoved her again. The dresser dug into her side. It hurt as much as his fingers digging into her arm. She dropped the phone, and it landed on the stack of papers.

Chester pushed her hand away, digging his fingers deeper into the skin. "Since you don't want to watch the show with your grandparents, go clean the kitchen. I'm sure they would appreciate that. Then if you're still bored, let me know and I'll find plenty more for you to do. Understand?"

Macy nodded, wincing from the pain.

"Answer me." He squeezed harder, this time, digging his nails into her flesh. She could feel it break the skin. Warm blood ran down her arm. She watched as several drops fell onto the pile of her clothes. "I said answer me!" He pulled her closer, grabbing her other arm. "Do you understand? Boredom will not be tolerated, you selfish, spoiled little brat."

Swallowing she nodded. "I understand."

"Don't be ungrateful for everything I've done for you."

She nodded, hating him even more than before. He had done nothing for her—nothing. Ripped her away from her family, forced her to eat meat, locked her in the back of his truck and then in the barn's dungeon, and then he had completely taken away her identity. She wasn't going to let him brainwash her. She would pretend if she had to, but deep down, she was going to hang onto every ounce of her dignity until she could get away from him.

He stepped back and shoved her toward the door, finally letting go of her arms. She rubbed them, glaring at him. How dare he? What made him think that he had the right to do all of this to her?

"Get out there and clean the kitchen for your grandparents. They're tired from their traveling."

She stared at him, wanting to give him a piece of her mind. Rubbing her arms, and thinking back over everything she'd been through in the last several days, she didn't think it was worth it. What if he put her back in the barn? She couldn't deal with that again.

"What are you waiting for?"

"Nothing."

He stepped toward her and grabbed her arm again. "You look like you have something to say. Say it."

"No. It's nothing."

A terrifying look covered his face. "Tell me."

"I don't want to."

"Too bad. You have to do what I say now, and I'm ordering you to tell me."

She stared at him, fear running through her. "Let me go. I want you to let me go."

He shoved her arm into her side. "I wasn't touching you when I first asked. That's not what you were going to say."

A lump formed in her throat as tears threatened. "Please stop."

"Please stop," he mocked her. He shoved her against the bed, her head hitting the post. "What were you going to say? Tell me."

Her heart raced. It didn't matter what she said, he would keep hurting her. If she lied, he would know. If she told him the truth, he would make her pay. "Let me go."

"Not until you tell me what you were going to say."

Tears filled her eyes. Macy stared at him with defiance. If she was going to tell him the truth, then he may as well know how much she meant it. "I want to go home."

"Home? You are home. At least for now, this is your home."

Macy's eyes widened. What did that mean?

He grabbed her shirt, bringing her close enough that she could smell him again. She gagged as she tried to pull herself from his grip. He tightened his hold on her collar. "This is home, and this is your only family. Those other people don't appreciate you the way we do. They're not your family. I brought you here to keep you safe. You need my protection. Only I can keep you safe. Those idiots couldn't find their own shadow in the middle of the summer."

"Don't talk about them like—"

He threw her into the bedpost. "Don't talk back to me ever again."

She turned around in time to see his fist headed right for her face. She raised her arms in defense, but didn't have enough time to block him. She heard a cracking noise as he made contact. Pain shot through her nose and then hot, thick liquid drained from it. She brought her hands to her nose, feeling the blood pool in her palms.

Chester shook his head. "Stupid girl. Look what you did."

What she had done?

He turned around and grabbed her gross clothes he had taken from the garbage. He shoved them into her arms. "May as well use these. You didn't want them anyway, did you?"

Macy grabbed them, wiping her nose. It burned on the inside, where the blood gushed from. It ran down into her throat, burning that as well. The awful, metallic taste made her gag as some of the blood made its way into her mouth.

By the time her nose stopped bleeding, the clothes were covered in blood. He snatched them out of her hands and threw them back on the floor. "Are you ready to start being grateful?"

She nodded, too angry to say anything.

"Good. Go in the bathroom and clean your face off."

"You broke my nose."

"Stop being dramatic." He felt her nose. "It's not broken. Bruised, sure, but I assure you it's not broken."

Macy rubbed it, glaring at him. Why did she have the feeling that he had enough practice with hitting people that he knew what he was talking about?

"Get in the bathroom. Your grandparents are going to wonder where we've gone."

Without thinking, she glared at him. "They're not my grandparents!"

A look of fury covered his face. His fist came at her face again. She tried to move out of the way, but was too late. She felt his knuckles make contact before everything went black.

Clothes

ALYSSA LOOKED AROUND her dark room, unsure what had woken her. She couldn't hear anything now. Rolling over, she saw that Chad wasn't in bed with her—of course. They were getting along, but he wouldn't leave his computer, afraid he would miss a comment on his blog saying they had found Macy.

Pain seared through her broken heart at the thought of her daughter. Where could Macy be? If she listened to what people had to say on the various shows, the likelihood of Macy still being alive was low. She looked at the time; it was after one in the morning. It had now been seven days since Macy had gone missing.

An entire week. Alyssa didn't know how she had survived those days. Everything was a horrible, heart-wrenching blur. Nothing was worse than not knowing where her child was. More than anything, all she wanted was to find Macy and hold her in her arms and never let go again.

Tears filled her eyes. Would she ever see Macy alive? Had she run away, or had something far more sinister happened? There was no evidence either way.

Her phone rang. Was that what had woken her up? She found it under her pillow and saw that she did have a missed call. She didn't recognize the number, but she didn't care. It could be someone with information about Macy.

"Hello? Who is this?"

"Mrs. Mercer, this is Officer Anderson. We have information about your daughter."

"What? Did you find her? Where is she? Where can I—?"

"Ma'am, please calm down."

Calm down? How dare he tell her to calm down? The only way she was going to calm down would be if Macy was back home, safe and sound. She grabbed a blanket and squeezed. "Go on."

"Some clothes have been found, and we need you and your husband to come down to the station and identify them."

Alyssa froze. Why did they think the clothes were Macy's? Where would she be without her clothes? It had to be a mistake—a horrible, horrible mistake.

"Mrs. Mercer, are you there?"

She gasped for air. "Yes. Where did they find them?"

"Near the mall."

"She could be close?"

"We can answer your questions at the station. Will you two be able to come down?"

"Of course. You want us to leave now?"

"The sooner the better, Ma'am. If they're identified as hers, we'll need to proceed as quickly as possible."

"What do they look like?"

"It would be better if you came here to see them."

The tone of his voice was enough to send chills through her. Something was wrong. "What aren't you telling me?"

"Really, it would—"

"What aren't you telling me?"

He sighed. "There is some blood on them."

Alyssa's throat closed up, and as it did an awful sound escaped. Blood on Macy's clothes? She shook her head as tears filled her eyes. "No."

"Ma'am? Do you need us to send someone to pick you up?"

She didn't want to be at their mercy, waiting to go back home until someone could drive them back. "We'll be there." She ended the call, taking deep breaths. She felt as though she was going to pass out. Bloody clothes? No. That wasn't right. It couldn't be. Macy had run off with a little punk from the Internet. A young, stupid teenager who didn't know the difference between a knife and a gun.

Her body felt like a lead weight. She couldn't move from the bed. She didn't *want* to get up. Seeing those clothes could be the end of her hope.

What if they were Macy's? And worse, what if they really *were* bloody?

Alyssa had never been particularly religious, but she had found herself praying a lot over the last week. Her stomach twisted in knots at the thought of it being that long. Alyssa put the phone on the headboard and grabbed an armful of blankets, clutching them tight. "God, please, *please* let Macy be alive and safe. Whatever happens with the blood, bring her back to us, alive."

Hot tears fell to her cheeks. She had to find a way to pull herself out of bed. She didn't want to face the fact that the clothes could be Macy's. What would that mean if they were? If it was bad, she didn't want to know. She would rather get back outside, searching for her.

Was that how the clothes had been found in the first place? The search team? Where had they been found? How? Alyssa felt a renewed sense of purpose. Even if the clothes were bloody, it could be a clue to finding Macy. What if she wasn't far from where the clothes had been found? What if Alyssa herself was the one to find and save her?

She jumped out of bed, nearly tripping over the blankets she had been hanging onto. "Macy, we're coming, baby. Hang on."

After she threw on some clothes, she ran downstairs to Chad's office. He was sleeping with his head on the desk again.

"Chad, wake up. We have to get to the police station. They might have a lead."

He sat up, making a snoring noise. He looked at Alyssa, obviously trying to process what she had said. "What? What kind of clue?"

"They found some clothes. They might be hers."

He rose from his chair, grabbing several things from the desk. "What makes them think that?"

"I don't know, but they want us to look at them. After we do, we need to go to wherever they found them and search with a fine-toothed comb. We're getting close. We can find her."

Panic covered his face. "But something has to be wrong. Why do they want us at this hour?"

"Because they don't want to waste any time, and neither do I. Let's go." She knew she should tell him about the blood, but she couldn't bring herself to say it. It would be like admitting defeat. They had to find their daughter.

Chad shook his head. "It's been a week. This can't be good. Did they say anything else?"

She twisted some of her hair around her fingers. "There was a little blood."

"On the clothes?" His eyes widened, and his face lost color.

Alyssa nodded. "We need to go. We don't even know if they're hers."

He sat in his chair, or possibly fell. Alyssa couldn't tell.

"Let's go. We need to go."

"Blood?"

"Chad, we have to look at the clothes. Whether they're hers or not, we need to find out."

He slammed his fist on the desk. "I'll hunt down the stupid bastard myself and beat him to a pulp. He'll wish he had never messed with our family." He stood again, grabbing his coat from the back of his chair.

They got into Chad's car, and as it roared to life the radio blared. "The case of missing Macy Mercer has grabbed our town by the heart. She's become everyone's daughter, even for those of us who never met her. I was talking to one of the people leading up the search party, and he—"

Alyssa turned it off. "I can't listen to that."

"Me neither." Chad pulled into the road and they drove in silence.

As they pulled into the parking lot, Alyssa asked, "Do you think the clothes are hers?"

"I have no idea. They could be anyone's. They could've fallen out of someone's gym bag."

"Someone's bloody gym bag?" Alyssa asked.

"It could happen."

After Chad set the alarm, he grabbed Alyssa's hand. "We're on the same team."

She nodded, feeling like a teenager herself, holding his hand as they walked through the lot. He had been holding her hand more since Macy disappeared, but it still felt unnatural.

When they got inside, they were whisked into a room with a dark plastic bag sitting in the middle of a table. The officer inside introduced himself as Anderson, the same one Alyssa had spoken to on the phone.

Alyssa stood, staring. "Are the clothes in there?"

The officer nodded. "Have a seat. We have some questions first, and then we'll have a look at the clothes."

She complied, but couldn't take her eyes off the bag. What were the clothes in there? Were they really Macy's?

"Ma'am?"

"What?" Alyssa turned to the cop.

"I have a few questions for you."

She nodded, and then answered some routine questions that she had already answered about fifty times since Macy disappeared. What was the point of asking the same questions over and over? Did that really do anything to help find Macy?

"Do you remember what she was wearing that night?" Anderson asked.

"Last I saw her, she was in her pajamas," Alyssa snapped. "She was tired from school—or so she said. Obviously, Zoey knows a lot more than I do. Didn't she describe what Macy was planning on wearing? We were out of the loop on that one. She didn't tell us she was sneaking out to meet someone she met on the Internet."

"I understand, Ma'am. We have to ask the questions to verify that the answers haven't changed."

She narrowed her eyes. "And why would they be different?"

"It's routine. Please, don't take it personally."

Alyssa heard Chad chuckle next her. She ignored him, keeping her attention on the officer. "Nothing has changed. We want to find our daughter. You brought us down here in the middle of the night, the least you can do is to show us the clothes."

Officer Anderson looked over his notes. "We've gone over everything we need to up to this point." He got up, walked over to the door, and opened it, poking his head out. He said something that sounded like gibberish to Alyssa. He came back in with not one, but two more policemen.

Did it really take five adults to look at a bag of clothes?

Chad stood. "Where were these found? And by who?"

Anderson put a hand up. "First things first, sir. This is Officer Reynolds and Detective Fleshman."

They all shook hands. Alyssa was certain that she would forget everyone's names, although she did recognize the two new men. "Can we see the clothes, please?"

Detective Fleshman walked to the bag, opening it slowly. Was he doing that on purpose? Alyssa thought she might explode. Dump everything out! What was he waiting for?

He held up a light blue camisole covered in blood.

Alyssa gasped. Chad wrapped an arm around her. "Is that Macy's?"

"I think so. But look at all that blood. Oh, dear God."

Reynolds looked at her. "You think it's hers? Or it *is* hers?"

"Macy wears those under her shirts all the time, but then again so do her friends. She's always liked that powder blue color. How would I know if it's hers? It could be anyone's." Tears filled her eyes. It was the right size. What would have happened to her baby to make her bleed like that?

Fleshman placed the camisole flat on the table, and then pulled out a black hoodie with little, red flowers all over it.

"Macy has one like that, but it has purple flowers," Alyssa said. Then it hit her: the flowers were covered in blood—that was why they were red. Her stomach lurched, and had she eaten anything the day before, it would have come up. "That's blood. It's covered!"

Chad held her tighter. She buried her face into his chest, sobbing.

"Where did you find the clothes?" Chad demanded.

"Near the mall," Anderson said. "By the jogging trail."

"What does this mean? Are you any closer to finding her? Will this help?"

"The next step will be to find out the blood is hers."

Alyssa sat up. "What do we do now?"

Fleshman gave her a sympathetic look. "Go home and get some sleep."

Dread

Zoey peeled some midnight-blue nail polish off her pinky nail. It had chipped badly, but she didn't care. Usually she kept her nails perfect, but with Macy gone, nothing seemed to matter anymore.

Her mom yawned next to her. "They call us down here at this ungodly hour, and then they make us wait. Not everyone works the graveyard shift." She glared at the officer sitting at the front desk.

He looked at them. "The girl's parents are looking at the clothes now. I'm sure it won't be much longer." He looked back at the computer screen in front of him.

"I'll bet he's playing games," muttered Zoey's mom.

"Do you want to go home, and I'll have one of them bring me back?"

Her face softened. "No, Zoey. Honey, I'm sorry. I'm so tired. I know this has been a hellish week for everyone. I'm here for you, and I'm not going to leave your side. If I have to miss work again tomorrow, then I will."

"Tomorrow's Saturday, Mom."

"Work hours don't make themselves up. It's going to take me a few weekends and evenings to make up the time I've already missed, and I'm sure to miss more. Don't worry about it."

Zoey rolled her eyes. Why would she worry about her mom's work schedule? She went back to picking at her nails, and her mom pulled out her tablet. Zoey ignored her, pretending that her nails were most interesting thing around. She wasn't even fooling herself, the one person she wanted to.

Her stomach churned acid. All this time she had told herself she was mad at Macy for running off with Jared, but deep down she knew that wasn't like her best friend. Her shy, vegan friend who often hid behind Zoey wouldn't run off with a guy she had just met. As nice as that would be to believe, it didn't make sense.

What did make sense was what they were waiting to see: clothes with blood on them. It couldn't be—not Macy. The last week had to have been one long sick and twisted nightmare. But if that was the case, why couldn't Zoey wake up?

Conversation caught her attention. Zoey sat up, forgetting about her nails. It sounded like Macy's parents. The voices got closer, until she could see them talking with a cop. They rounded a corner, entering the waiting area.

Zoey stood up. Where was Alex? Did they leave him home? In a way, she was jealous. She wished she could get sleep instead of waking from nightmares constantly. Her dreams wouldn't leave her alone, always reminding her of what she was truly afraid of. She had woken up from almost every scenario possible: Macy being shot, stabbed, poisoned, strangled, hanged, drugged, and more.

Alyssa turned their way. Mascara streaked down her face, and her eyes were red and puffy. She had obviously been crying—a lot. Zoey's heart sank. Why were they even there? The clothes had probably already been identified as Macy's from the looks of it.

Her mom got up and gave Macy's parents both a hug. Nobody spoke about the clothes or Macy.

When Alyssa made eye contact with Zoey, she nodded. "Thanks for coming down here, Zo. You've always been such a good friend to…." Tears fell down her face, further smearing the mascara.

Zoey looked away, afraid that she would cry too.

Chad caught her attention. "We do appreciate you, Zoey. Both of you." He looked at her mom. "If you guys ever need anything, let us know."

"I'm the one who should be offering you something, Chad."

"Where's Alex?" Zoey blurted out.

Her mom glared at her. They both knew she couldn't help it, though. When she was uncomfortable, her mouth did its own thing.

"Oh, Alex!" Alyssa's eyes widened, and her lips wobbled. "I'm the worst mother ever. Macy is gone and we left without Alex."

Zoey's mom shot her a dirty look and turned to Alyssa. Zoey sighed. How was she supposed to know Alyssa would get even more upset?

"Alyssa, I'm sure he's better off at home, sleeping. You guys have been through enough."

"But we didn't even think to check on him! I forgot all about him when I got that phone call. I'm not—"

"He probably won't even know you're gone."

Alyssa looked at her. "But, Valerie, I forgot about my son. I forgot about him!" More tears fell, and she wiped at them, spreading the mascara sideways. Zoey wished she had something she could give her to wipe it all off.

The officer behind the desk called Zoey and her mom back. They said their goodbyes to the Mercers and followed him to a room with nothing except a table, chairs, and a black bag.

Three policemen came in, introducing themselves as Anderson, Reynolds, and Fleshman. Zoey let her mom do all the talking. She enjoyed being in charge and quickly dominated the conversation.

Zoey stared at the black bag, curious and disgusted at the same time. She wasn't sure if she wanted to run away or look at the clothes.

Before she knew it, one of the cops grabbed the bag. Zoey jumped, startled. She'd been so lost in her own thoughts she hadn't been paying attention to anything being said.

"Why are we here? Didn't Macy's parents just see the clothes?"

Her mom sighed. "Didn't you listen to anything they said?"

Fleshman said, "It's okay. We know it's a stressful time." He turned to Zoey. "With you being her best friend, you might be able to offer additional insight that her parents couldn't."

Zoey shrugged. How could she help? She didn't know anything.

The detective pulled out Macy's pants. Zoey recognized them right away. They had spent hours at the mall looking for pants. Macy didn't like any of the ones she had, saying they were too out of style. Zoey thought her pants were fine, but she knew how cruel some of the popular girls had been to Macy.

"Do you recognize these?"

Holding her breath, Zoey nodded. She took a slow, deep breath, trying to control herself. “She bought those for her date.” Zoey slunk down into a chair. She covered her face with her hands, not wanting anyone to see her cry. She had held herself together up to that point, but seeing the pants was too much.

Her mom was talking with the cops. She didn’t want to hear any more. She was done. She sat up. “Can I go now? I told you those are her pants.”

Fleshman walked around the table and put his hand on her shoulder. “We really need you to look at the rest of them. Can you do that much for us? For Macy?”

She sighed. “Fine.” She took a deep breath, determined to keep herself together. The pants hadn’t had any blood on them. Maybe the police had only mentioned blood to get them down there at two in the morning.

One of the other cops pulled out Macy’s favorite hoodie. Why were the flowers red? The blood drained from her face. “Is that blood?” Without thinking, she grabbed the hoodie. It crunched in her grasp. “Is that Macy’s blood?”

“We don’t know yet. It’s going to take some time to process. We wanted to have the clothes identified first because we have to send them to a larger department that has those capabilities.”

Zoey dropped the hoodie onto the table. “It’s hers, like the pants. Can I go now?” The room spun around her. She wanted to get out.

Anderson pulled out Macy’s new camisole, which was covered in blood.

A foreign sound escaped from Zoey’s throat. “I gave that to her for her birthday. Her old one was too big after she lost weight.” She sat back down in the chair. How much more of this would she have to endure? They showed her socks, but Zoey didn’t know if they were Macy’s.

Zoey waited for them to bring out underwear and a bra, but they didn’t. Was that a good thing?

“Where did you find these?” Valerie asked.

“A jogger found them near the mall.”

“That’s where she was supposed to meet him.” Zoey felt lightheaded. “They were just supposed to go to the mall.”

One of the cops looked at her. "But that area had been gone over. The clothes weren't there a couple days ago."

"Does that mean she's close?" Zoey sat up, hopeful. "We've got to find her."

Fleshman shook his head. "The clothes appeared to have been placed there. There wasn't a sign of struggle or anything else suspicious. We had some dogs brought in, and they couldn't detect a thing."

What could it all mean? Zoey looked at each of the cops. None of them appeared to know more than she did.

"When will you know whose blood that is?" Valerie asked.

"It could be as long as a week. We're going to request they make it a priority, but it's not our department. We can only hope they'll comply since it's a missing child case."

Zoey ran her hands through her hair, not caring how much she messed it up. She had to get out of there. The walls were closing in on her. Her eyes were also getting heavy. She needed to get some sleep, even if it was riddled with `nightmares. Her eyes closed, giving into their weight.

She drifted off to sleep right away. Images of bloody clothes filled her dreams. Somewhere, Macy was calling for help.

"Zoey, we're leaving now."

Not wanting to move, she pretended not to hear her mom. She didn't care that she was sleeping in a chair down at the station. At least she was sleeping.

"Come on, Zoey. You can sleep in the car."

She mumbled something that not even she understood.

"A little help, please?"

Zoey felt hands slide under her legs and around her back. She had the vague awareness of being carried. Good. She didn't feel like opening her eyes or walking.

Bound

MACY OPENED HER eyes, but it was just as dark as when they were closed. She looked around, trying to see anything. Was she back in Heather's room? Something covered her mouth. Macy moved her mouth back and forth. It felt like duct tape.

She went to sit up, but couldn't move. What was going on? She moved her arms, but they wouldn't budge. She tried her legs next, and they were stuck, too. She wiggled around, feeling pressure around her wrists, ankles, and knees. Was she tied up?

Her hair rested on her cheek, making it itch. She moved her head to scratch the itch with her shoulder. Instead, she scratched her face on something hard, breaking the skin. She moved her head around, feeling a poking sensation along her face.

No.

She was back in the barn. She was lying on hay. She looked around again, hoping to see something as her eyes adjusted to the dark. She couldn't make anything out. Not a single shape. It had to be really late, unless her eyes had been covered too.

Squirming, she managed to get her shoulder up to her face. Something was wrapped around her eyes. It could be the middle of the day for all she knew.

She could hear hooves up above. If she'd doubted she was back in the dungeon, those doubts were gone. She could hear the rodents moving around in the room somewhere.

What could she do? George and Ingrid were on the farm. If she screamed, they would hear her if they were near the barn. If they found her, she could tell them everything. They could call the police and get her home.

On the other hand, Chester could hear her screaming and make things even worse for her.

She didn't care. It was worth the risk. She had to take it.

Macy took a deep breath, preparing herself to yell louder than she ever had before. She let out the loudest, bone-curdling scream she could muster. It barely made a sound because of the duct tape.

Her stomach growled. How long had she been back in the dungeon? More importantly, how much longer would she be there? She had to find a way out this time. Although it would clearly be more challenging now that she was bound up.

The last thing she was going to do was to wallow in her misery. She needed to find a way to get herself free. She couldn't tell for sure, but it felt like zip ties were wrapped around her wrists and ankles. They were skinny and tight, painfully digging into her flesh. He probably made them too tight on purpose. He wanted her to pay for talking back to him.

Did he seriously believe that he was doing her a favor? That she was lucky? He might have hoped that tying her up and sticking her back in the barn would make her need him more, but it had backfired. She was pissed off, and after she freed herself she would attack him when he came back for her.

He would regret ever taking her. Strike that. He would regret ever having seen her online in the first place. She had seen enough of Alex's karate to put some of it to use. She wished she had paid more attention, or even taken lessons herself, instead of texting and playing games, but it wasn't like she could have predicted that she would end up kidnapped.

Stupid jerk. He was going to pay. She wiggled and squirmed. No matter what it took, she was going to get up, and then she would find a way to free herself. As she fought to sit upright, she pictured the dungeon. In her mind's eye, she looked around for anything she could use to free herself.

Nothing came to mind, but she would have to find something. A sharp piece of wood sticking out from a wall, maybe. There had to be something.

As she continued to wiggle around, the hay scratched up her arms and face. She wasn't even sure if she had moved at all. When she had watched shows with someone tied up, she thought it had been over-dramatized. Now it seemed under-done. She wasn't getting anywhere, and she was starting to break out into a sweat.

The cloth over her eyes was collecting moisture and feeling heavier. Macy continued to fight, but no matter how much she struggled, she didn't get anywhere.

Her throat was dry, and she had to go to the bathroom. She had to find a way out of the restraints, if for no other reason than to relieve herself. With more fight than before, she struggled to get off the bale. Maybe she could at least try to stand up. Then she could find something—anything—to break the zip ties.

Her bladder burned, especially as she moved around. With each movement, it protested. She finally made some progress and rolled onto her stomach.

Tears of joy escaped. If she managed to roll over once, she could do it again. She moved her head to the side, getting her face out of the bale.

The pressure on her bladder was too much. She wasn't going to be able to hold it until she could get the ties off and her pants down.

No. Please.

Her burning bladder was all she could focus on. She had to go so bad. New tears ran down out of her eyes, soaking the blindfold.

She was about to pee herself, she knew it was only a matter of minutes, if that. She squeezed her muscles together to keep it in, squirming and rolling with as much force as she could. She rolled again, feeling a strange sensation. She was falling. It felt further than one bale. How far was she going to fall?

Thud. She landed flat on her back. She let out a cry, and then her bladder released its contents. Warm liquid ran through her pants, puddling around her.

Macy stayed in place, crying again. More than before, she wanted to get home. Back to her family. *If I ever get back, I swear I will appreciate them. I'll do what I'm supposed to.*

She stayed there, making promises into the duct tape until the puddle around her went cold. Her stomach growled again, but the smell of her urine made her gag.

Shivers ran through her. It was getting cold, and being in a puddle wasn't helping anything. Having learned a little bit about rolling over while restrained, she was able to roll over onto her side easier than she had before.

It felt like hours had passed since she woke up. How long was he going to leave her down there? Her blood ran cold as the most horrible thought struck: what if he had left her down there to die? Was he looking for a new Heather even now?

Macy knew his name and his parents' names. She could easily describe the barn and the farmhouse. She was a risk for him to let go if he had decided she was too much trouble.

Fresh determination ran through her. She had to get out of the barn—alive. She didn't care what it took; she was going to find a way out and then get home. She didn't care if she was clear across the country. She would do it somehow.

The first thing she had to do was to roll until she hit something, preferably a wall. Then she would find a board to rub against the zip tie holding her arms together. She ignored her drenched, cold pants and rolled herself over again.

She was getting tired and she was still hungry and thirsty. She knew she could go about three days without water, but she didn't even know how long it had been already.

No matter what it would take, she *would* get out and back to her family.

Reminders

CHAD PULLED HIS arm away from Alyssa. She had finally fallen asleep after insisting that he hold her. She had been so upset with herself for forgetting about Alex when they left for the station.

Alex would have figured they left him to sleep. The poor kid hadn't had much rest himself the last week, and the last thing Chad had wanted was for his son to have to deal with seeing Macy's clothes. Alex was already upset enough about her disappearance.

Alex was just like Chad, keeping his feelings to himself, but Chad could read him like a book. He could see that Macy's disappearance was eating Alex up.

Sitting up, he fixed the blankets around Alyssa. Even though it was late and he was exhausted, he couldn't sleep. How could he after seeing his daughter's bloody clothes?

Chad knew enough about blood loss to know that the amount on the clothes wasn't enough to kill her. It was more like a cut. A bad one, but not enough to be fatal.

A sick feeling settled into his stomach. How could anyone do that to his daughter? He would personally hunt down the one responsible and beat him within an inch of his life. He would find out what he did to Macy, and then he would do exactly the same thing to the sick bastard.

Maybe someone had posted something on his blog. Since her clothes had been found, maybe more evidence would pop up, too. The traffic to his blog had more than quadrupled over the last week. In fact, it had received so much traffic that it had shut down for a while. He had to pay for more hosting because his plan couldn't handle it.

He couldn't afford to let it be down. What if someone had news about Macy?

Knowing that his family would probably think he was a jerk, he got up out of bed and went down to his office. It was for Macy, no matter what they thought about him being on his blog. It was to help her.

At least with the blog, he could give his side of the story. He was able to let everyone know what his family was really like. He posted pictures that the news wanted nothing to do with. Ironically, those were the ones that the blog visitors loved the most.

His broken heart hurt even more knowing he couldn't call his dad. When he had been alive, Chad had been able to call him any time he needed to talk. What would Dad tell him? Probably to fight for Macy. That was what he had to do.

Chad climbed out of bed, careful not to wake Alyssa. He grabbed her phone from the headboard and took it with him downstairs. People called around the clock these days, and he didn't want anyone waking her.

He went to his office and went straight to his laptop. In another situation, he would have been thrilled looking at the numbers. He had more comments than he had time to read. The page views were unlike anything he had ever seen, even the day before. All those people cared about Macy.

He pulled the chair up and went to his comments. He read through them, answering each one. When he looked up to check the time, he saw that three and a half hours had already passed. It was getting light out. The house was still silent, which meant that Alex and Alyssa were both getting the sleep they needed.

His eyes were getting heavy. As much as he wanted to write a post, he knew he didn't have it in him to write a good enough one. Macy deserved better, and so did the people reading the posts.

There also wasn't much to report, since he wasn't supposed to say anything about the clothes. If people were really interested in what he had to say, they would read his replies to all the comments.

People would stop visiting if he didn't get a new post up soon. His vision was blurry, and his body ached. Surely they would understand and could wait a few hours. His neck and shoulders were sore from so many hours spent sleeping against his desk or on the couch.

He got up and went up to his room, sliding in bed next to Alyssa. She didn't even stir. The moment his head hit the pillow, he was asleep.

When he woke up, Alyssa was gone. He looked around, listening. The sun was bright, slipping in through the blinds. He felt rested. How long had he slept? It had to be after noon. He climbed out of bed and went to the bathroom, noting Alyssa's makeup spread around her side of the counter.

She hadn't put on makeup since she found out about Macy. However much sleep she had gotten must have helped to get her in a better frame of mind. He checked on Alex and found his bed empty too. He searched the house, but they weren't anywhere. They had probably gone to search for Macy.

He should probably join them, but first he needed to check his blog. His stomach rumbled as he passed the kitchen. He looked inside, knowing it would be bare. Shopping hadn't been on anyone's priority list. Alex was the only one eating regularly.

Chad grabbed the last frozen burrito and stuck it in the microwave. He had always wanted to try to order groceries online. Maybe he could try that while he checked his blog. Then at least there would be food in the house for his family. The microwave beeped, and he took his food out. He found a clean fork and headed for his office.

The computer was ready for him. Two hundred and fifteen new comments. How long had he been asleep? That was an unheard of amount of comments in that amount of time. He should order the groceries first. By the time he was done with the comments, they would be delivered.

Once at their grocery store's site, he created a login and filled a virtual shopping cart with items he was pretty sure they usually had on hand. He threw in a few things that he thought Alex and Alyssa would like that they rarely had, and then he checked out. It would be at their door in two hours. He wanted to join the search party before that, but it might take that long to get through all those comments.

Up until this point, he had replied to every comment ever left on his blog—excluding the spam comments which he removed as soon as he saw them. He didn't need their links ruining his ranking. He wouldn't have been able to get the advertisers he had if he allowed crap like that on his site.

He readjusted himself in the chair, making himself as comfortable as possible. The first comment was someone expressing their heartfelt sympathy for their loss. It sounded like they thought Macy was dead.

Most of them were similar, saying something along the lines of being sorry for Macy being gone. Many said they were praying for her safe return. No one had mentioned anything about the clothes. He really had expected someone to leak the information and for the news to eat it up. Surely they would once they found out.

Before he knew it, the groceries had arrived. He put them away as best as he could. He didn't know where anything went, but at least they had food and the perishables were in the fridge and freezer. Nothing was going to spoil.

There were some more comments left unanswered, but he would have to get to them later. He found a baseball cap and put it on, not wanting to deal with a shower. He needed to get out there and join his family. The headquarters for the search parties had been at the park down the street over the past week, so he would walk.

As soon as he got to the sidewalk, he could see the temporary tents that had been set up. It looked like as much effort had been put into this search as the ones last weekend. He moved the bill of his hat to get all of the sun off his face. It was warm out, especially given that it was almost winter.

A few people milled around the park. They were handing out fliers. Chad saw a couple of women standing near a table full of supplies. One of them saw him and waved as he entered the park. He waved back and made his way to the table.

One lady he recognized from the homeowners' association smiled. "Chad, it's so good to see you. We all appreciate you updating your blog so often. We were talking about that a little while ago."

Another one nodded. "We love the pictures. They make us feel like we know you guys better, you know?"

He nodded. "Thanks. Did Alyssa and Alex come by? They left while I was sleeping."

The first woman nodded. "They went out with a search team near the mall. She said you hadn't been sleeping much, so they wanted you to get some rest. I can't even imagine what it's been like for you."

Chad cleared his throat. "Thanks. So, am I too late?"

She shook her head. "No. Parties have been coming and going all day. It shouldn't be long before another group arrives. We've got people canvassing with fliers and others out searching. We're going to do everything we can until she's found."

The second lady looked behind him. "Here comes a group now."

Chad spun around. He saw five people walking toward them. They came to the table. Each one recognized him and gave their condolences. He hated it. Macy was missing, not dead. Three of the group had to leave, and another to rest. That left someone he knew all too well.

Lydia.

She gave him a hug. "So many people have been working hard all day. Someone will find Macy. I can feel it."

He nodded, trying not to make direct eye contact. "Thanks."

One of the ladies from the table handed him a stack of fliers. "Why don't you two go hand out more of these? It's going to be dark soon."

Chad looked at Lydia. "I'm not sure—"

She grabbed the pile of papers. "Let's go." She took two water bottles from the table and handed him one. "We can't let these fliers go to waste."

He couldn't argue with that. They left the park in the opposite direction of his house.

"What are you doing, Lydia?" Chad asked.

"Helping to find Macy. What else?"

"Look. We're out of everyone's earshot. What are you really doing?"

She gave him a wounded look. "Helping to find your daughter."

"Lydia, we can't continue…what we had going."

"Haven't you noticed me giving you space? I haven't even tried to contact you in the last week. Although, I hope you know that if you do need to get away, I'm here for you day or night."

"Alyssa and I have been trying to work things out."

She kept her face straight, but he could see the hurt in her eyes. She flipped her hair behind her shoulder. "Of course. You two need to work together now. Alex needs you two strong more than ever."

"Yes. I know." He looked forward, not wanting to look at her. Now that he and Alyssa were getting along, and especially with Macy being gone, he regretted ever hooking up with Lydia. It was a mistake, and guilt ate at him. He had nearly forgotten all about her as soon as he found out about Macy being gone.

It was obvious Lydia wasn't going to go away. Why else would she be so active in the search efforts? She was obviously trying to show him that she was still there for him…and would be waiting.

"I can't imagine your pain. I've been reading your blog. It's beautiful. You have such a way with words. You're going to be a full-time writer soon. Then you're dream—"

"Lydia." Chad raked his fingers through his hair. "I'm trying to turn my marriage around."

"Chad, I'm not going to put any pressure on you. Honestly, I can't even fathom the hell you're going through. You know Dean and I never could have kids. I—"

"Where is Dean? Why aren't you out with him?"

"He's working. What else? It's a day that ends in 'y,' you know."

Chad nodded. They had both been lonely in their marriages, and that was what got them talking in the first place. One conversation had led to another, until one day they found themselves fulfilling each other's needs in other ways.

"I'm sorry he still has his head up his rear. You don't deserve that, but I can't replace him any more."

Her eyes shone with tears and she cleared her throat and adjusted her shirt which could have been buttoned higher. "I know you need this time with your family. I'm not going to bother you, but when you're ready to come back—and you will—I'll be waiting."

Chad looked around and seeing no one, he took her hand. "Lydia, you deserve better than Dean. You should find someone who can treat you well."

"That's why I'm going to wait for you as long as I need to."

"Please don't. It's over." He let go of her hand. "Let's hand these fliers out."

They rounded a corner and came face to face with Alyssa and Alex.

Spiral

ZOEY STOOD BY herself at the park only a few feet away from the others. They had just arrived after handing out the last flier. She kept her focus on Lydia. Something was off about her, but Zoey couldn't tell what. She looked perfectly normal, holding the stack of fliers and a water bottle, but she looked a little too comfortable standing next to Chad. Her shirt was also too low-cut for a search party.

Alyssa smiled at Lydia. "We appreciate you putting together the search parties. Really, we couldn't have asked for anything more. The fliers are perfect, and I think every inch of our neighborhood has been looked through."

Lydia smiled. "Glad to help. In the last HOA meeting, we were talking about other ways we can help your family. We want to do more." She stepped a little closer to Chad.

Zoey narrowed her eyes. She knew Macy wouldn't like it. She looked at Alyssa, who seemed oblivious to Lydia's behavior. Granted, Lydia was being subtle, but *something* was going on.

"If you guys need anything else, say the word." Lydia smiled again. Why was she smiling so much? She was talking to two parents who couldn't find their child.

Alyssa nodded. "Thanks. I'm going back home. You'll be home soon?" She looked at Chad.

"Sure. I need to get out and look for her myself."

"I'd join you, but I'm exhausted. Someone told me how we can try to recover the information from Macy's computer. It might still be there. Maybe we'll find something useful."

Chad put his hand on Alyssa's arm. "I'll help you when I get home. I shouldn't be too much longer."

Alyssa threw herself into his arms. "Thank you. I don't know much about computers. I don't want to mess it up and accidentally delete anything."

"Just go home and rest. I'll come back when we've handed out all these." He indicated to the stack of fliers in Lydia's hand.

Zoey didn't like the look on Lydia's face. She was tired from all the walking and drained from Macy's disappearance, but she wasn't going to let Lydia spend time alone with Macy's dad. Macy wouldn't have wanted that. Lydia had her eyes on Chad; there was no denying that.

Zoey grabbed Alex's hand. "We'll join you, Mr. Mercer. That way you guys can hand those out faster."

He looked relieved. Maybe he could tell something was up with Lydia, too.

Valerie looked at Zoey. "Are you sure? I know you're really tired."

"Yeah. It won't take long."

"Okay." Valerie turned to Alyssa. "I'll tell you what. While you're working on the computer, I'll make dinner for you guys. You probably haven't had a decent meal all week, have you?"

"Nope," Alex said.

Valerie turned to Lydia. "That's what the homeowners' association should do to help. These guys need to eat. Someone should make them meals. Dinners, at least."

Lydia grinned, grating further on Zoey's nerves. "That's a great idea. I'll take tomorrow."

Chad's eyes widened. Zoey wondered if maybe there wasn't something more going on other than just Lydia having the hots for Mr. Mercer. After all, Macy's parents hadn't been getting along for a while.

Zoey's mom and Macy's mom waved and then headed for the park, which they had to go through to get to their street. Zoey talked about everything they had done all day while canvassing, not letting Lydia get a word in edgewise.

Every once in a while, Alex would give her a strange look, but she didn't want to tell him what she was thinking. What if she was wrong? Her mom always said she had an overactive imagination. With everything else going on in Alex's life, she didn't want to give him something else to worry about.

She knew he was tired from walking all day, and neither of them had been sleeping well. Their frequent middle of the night texts proved that. They never really texted about Macy, but that was why they were both awake. Sometimes, it was nice to pretend that wasn't why they were awake.

They made their way around, handing out papers to everyone they came across. The further they went, the more Zoey's legs ached. Not only her legs, but her entire body. Maybe she would actually get some sleep tonight—if the dreams didn't disturb her.

Even though she was tired, she kept her eyes on Chad and Lydia. Zoey really wanted to be wrong about Lydia. This would have been the worst time for someone to go after either of Macy's parents.

When they got back to the park after handing out all of the fliers, Zoey was ready to drop. She could tell that Alex was, too. He looked about ready to pass out.

Lydia and Chad were talking with the people at the main table. Alex looked at Zoey. "Want to go back? It's getting dark."

She looked over at Alex's dad. He was standing a good two feet away from Lydia. "All right. You look like you need to sleep. I'm sure my mom has dinner ready by now."

He nodded, and then turned to his dad. "Hey, Dad. We're going back to the house now."

"I'll go with you two." He turned to the adults and waved a goodbye. They started the short trek back to the Mercer house. Normally it was a short walk, but after the day's searching it felt much longer.

No one spoke. Zoey wanted to know what Chad was thinking, but given the look of relief on his face when Zoey said she would go with him and Lydia, he was probably innocent. Lydia was probably going after him because he was weak. Or maybe she saw some kind of opportunity.

Or maybe Zoey was so desperate for something other than Macy to think about that she was making something out of nothing.

When they got to the front yard, Zoey felt like collapsing on the lawn, but forced her feet to keep going. Within the front door, a delicious smell greeted her. She guessed dinner was ready. She kicked her shoes off out of habit, feeling at home, and went to use the bathroom. She hadn't realized how bad she had to go until then.

By the time she got to the table, everyone else had already sat. Zoey took the seat next to Alex. Dinner smelled like herbs and chicken; her mouth watered. It had been Macy's favorite whenever she spent the night, at least before she went vegan. There were so many nights that they had eaten that meal and then ran up the stairs, giggling and whispering secrets.

Zoey's chest tightened as she thought about her best friend. What would she do without her? Tears filled her eyes as she filled her plate, not looking at anyone.

The discussion was light, mostly the Mercer's thanking Valerie for making the meal. The three of them scarfed down their food. Had they eaten since Macy disappeared?

After everyone had eaten, Zoey's mom made eye contact with her. "Will you help me with the dishes?"

"Sure."

Valerie looked at everyone else. "You guys get some rest. We'll take care of the kitchen."

They all said their thanks and went off in various directions. Zoey felt a little more energized after having eaten. She picked up the plates, stacking them on top of one another.

"I hate to do this to you, Zo, but my work needs me to travel to China for a few days. I feel bad about leaving you, and I wish I could be here for Macy's family, but this way I can catch up on my lost work hours. I can't afford to lose my job, honey. We don't want to lose the house."

Zoey put the plates on the counter. "What does that mean for me?"

"I know you could probably stay home and be fine, but I would feel better if you didn't. Would you be willing to stay here? Alyssa already said you were more than welcome. But if you don't want to stay in Macy's house, I understand. We can ask another of your friends' parents."

Her mom was offering for her to spend the night at Alex's house for a few days? "Here is fine."

"There's more." Her mom sighed. "You're not going to want to hear it, but I want you to."

"What?"

"I want you to go back to school on Monday."

"What? Mom—"

"Zoey, hear me out, I said. I don't want you falling behind, and you've already missed a week of school. They also have counselors there who are already talking with students, helping them deal with Macy's disappearance. I was told that you can go and talk with one at any time. They have extras on hand because so many kids want to talk about it. You would have priority, being her best friend."

"Kids are talking to counselors about her? Most of the kids made fun of her, and didn't stop even after she lost her weight."

Her mom's face became sad. "Those kids might be the ones who need to talk to someone the most. They might have a lot of guilt."

"They should! They're the ones who forced her into finding a boyfriend online. I hope those snarky bi—"

"Language, Zoey."

"Ugh." She rolled her eyes. "I'm not going to sugarcoat the truth. They're complete and total b—"

"Enough. Do you want to stay here? And are you willing to go to school? At least try it on Monday. If it's too much, we can have the teachers send work home."

"Sounds like you've really thought about this."

Valerie nodded. "Alyssa and I have been talking. She wants Alex to go back to school, too."

"I can't imagine he wants to go back any more than I do, but if Alex goes, I'll go."

"You might be the one to lead the way for him, Zo. I know he's Macy's kid brother and he probably annoys you, but I see the way he looks at you. He looks up to you. You have an opportunity here to make a difference in his life. His parents are overwhelmed with grief, so they're limited in what they can give him."

"Okay, I'll go to school for Alex."

"And you'll stay here?"

"For Alex."

Valerie hugged her. "Thank you, honey. I know it's really hard on you too."

Despite the grief, Zoey couldn't stop a smile tugging at her mouth. She was going to spend the night at Alex's house.

Stranger

ZOEY TOSSED AND turned in Macy's bed. As tired as she was, it was too weird being in her best friend's room. Sure, Zoey had been in the room countless times, and it had always felt like her second home. But with Macy being gone, she didn't feel right being there.

She sat up, looking around the room. Macy loved night-lights, and there were enough of them around the room that Zoey could see everything. The desk looked bare with the computer gone.

Would Macy really know how to return it to factory settings? She always called Zoey when she had to do something on her computer. Macy knew nothing about computers aside from turning them on and starting up the Internet and a couple of programs she needed for school. Zoey was no computer whiz, but she often felt like one compared to Macy.

Sure, it was possible that Macy had Googled directions, but she wouldn't have been able to follow them. It didn't make any sense that she would have wiped the computer clean before leaving.

What if Jared had done that? He had removed his social media profiles, so it would stand to reason that if he had done something with Macy that he could have reset her computer. How would they have gotten into the house? It had been Macy's first time sneaking out. She wouldn't have sneaked back in with him, would she?

There were too many things that didn't add up, and again, she came back to the fact that Macy wouldn't ignore her. If Macy ran off with Jared, Zoey would have been the first to know. Even if it was only a quick text. She would have let Zoey know something.

She needed a cigarette. There was no way to sneak out onto the roof from Macy's room. It was a steep drop, and she wasn't stupid enough to risk it. If Chad and Alyssa were sleeping, she could go into the back yard. If they were awake, she would have to get creative. She really needed one.

Zoey got out of bed as quiet as possible, threw on a hoodie and then slid a pack and a lighter into the pocket. She opened the bedroom door and jumped when she saw Chad standing next to her, just outside the room, looking to the side. "Mr. Mercer, you startled me."

Wait. Why was he wearing a baseball cap and sunglasses, with his hoodie pulled on top of his head?

He turned and looked at her. Chad didn't have over-sized glasses, bushy eyebrows or a beard. A nine o'clock shadow, sure, but nothing like what this guy had.

Zoey's heart dropped. "You're not Mr. Mercer."

"And you shouldn't be in Heather's room."

"What? Who's Hea—?"

The man grabbed her, covering her mouth before she could scream. Zoey hit and kicked him, fighting even harder as he tightened his grip. He pinned her arms to her body. She kicked even harder, trying to bruise his shins. She couldn't scream, so she tried to bite him, but she couldn't even get her mouth open.

He moved his finger to block her nose. He was trying to kill her. Struggling to breathe, she continued to kick. She tried elbowing him, but she couldn't move her arms. Her fingers were free, so she pinched his legs on both sides. He let out a gasp and swore at her, shoving his finger further against her nose.

Zoey felt dizzy. She kept kicking his shins and squirmed with all her might. If she could squirm enough, maybe she could loosen his hold and get away. It was her only hope. She couldn't breathe, and she was getting dizzier by the second. It made it harder to fight him.

His grip on her tightened. She kept kicking and squirming, but suddenly she couldn't keep it up. She couldn't think straight, and her vision went dark.

When Zoey woke up, she was cold. Where was she? She blinked several times, but it was too dark to see anything. She got the shivers. She was on a cold floor. She stood up, banging her head against something metal. The floor was especially cold on her feet. Where were her socks? Hadn't she gone to bed with socks on?

She stopped. She had gone to bed in Macy's room. What happened after that? Everything flooded back into her memory. That man hadn't killed her after all.

Where was she?

Desperation filled her, and she forgot about how cold she was. She felt around, walking as quietly as she could.

If he was nearby, the last thing she wanted to do was let him know she was awake. Zoey's hand touched what she was sure was a car. She kept her hand on it, walking alongside it. When she got to the other end, she felt around for something else she could use to guide her.

There was nothing in her reach, so she continued along, following the car. Why was it so dark? Was it still night? Were there no windows in this…whatever the place was? A garage, maybe. Hopefully that meant she wasn't being watched. Chills ran down her back as she pictured that guy watching her with night vision goggles. Again with her overactive imagination.

She picked up speed, eager to get out of the garage. She felt around the air as she walked, and eventually found a table or some kind of bench. It might have been Chad's tool bench. It was right where it should be if she was in their garage and she was walking alongside Alyssa's car. If she followed the bench to the other side, she should get to the door leading to the house.

More than anything, she needed to get inside to the Mercers. What if he had done something to them? She picked up her speed, praying that she wouldn't find them all in pools of their own blood.

Zoey felt along the bench until she reached the end. She walked to where the door should have been and found the handle. Holding her breath, she turned it. The door opened with a low squeak. The inside of the house was lighter than the garage, and as her eyes adjusted she could see she was in the Mercers' downstairs.

Before running up the stairs, she listened for any sounds. Everything was silent. It was too quiet, in fact. All kinds of bloody images flooded her mind. She had to get up to Alex's room to make sure he was okay. She ran up the stairs, unable to get images of an ax jammed in his head out of her mind. All she could imagine was his dead body lying in his blood-soaked bed.

By the time she reached the hall leading to the bedrooms, she had herself convinced that Alex was dead. Tears ran down her face. He was dead, she knew it. Two of the most important people in her life were gone.

She threw open his door and turned the light on. She didn't see any blood—she couldn't see anything for a moment. The light was blinding until her eyes adjusted. The first thing she noticed was Alex covering his head with a pillow.

"Turn it off. It's too bright." His voice was muffled.

Zoey let out a sigh of relief. He was alive. She turned the light off and leaned against the wall, gasping for air. She hadn't realized she had been holding her breath until she released it.

"What's going on?"

She ran to his bed, throwing herself against him, into his arms. "I'm so glad you're alive."

"Why wouldn't I be? What's going on?"

Snuggling closer, she found his face and gave him a prolonged kiss.

He returned the kiss for a moment, but then pulled away. "Why are you so upset?"

"I'm so glad you're alive," she repeated.

"Why?" He sounded out of breath. Alex pulled his head back and looked at her. They could barely see each other from what little light was coming through the window.

"I don't want to talk about it."

"You have to. Why are you so freaked out?"

She frowned, sighing. He was right. Even though she didn't want to talk about it, she needed to. She was still shaking. "I was going to go out for a smoke, but then I ran into someone in the hall."

"My parents?"

"No."

"What do you mean? Who?" Color drained from his face.

She leaned her head against his shoulder and then told him the entire story, shaking. Zoey left out the part about him calling Macy Heather. It was too weird, and it was a stupid detail, wasn't it?

Alex wrapped his arms around her, holding her tight. "Are you okay?"

"I am now. I was so afraid he had gotten to you. I was way more worried about you than anything else."

He looked her in the eyes. "We need to get my parents."

She shook her head. "No. I don't want to talk about it again."

"You have to tell them everything you told me. Some guy broke in here, Zoey. He could have hurt you worse than he did. What if he's still in here? Or if he took something? What if he comes back?"

Fear washed over her. "Just hold me."

He pulled her closer. "We still need to tell them. It's for all of our safety. Somehow he got in even though we have a security system. That's not good. You said you're worried about me, right?"

She nodded. "I was so scared I lost you. I can't lose you. I can't." She clung to him.

"Then you have to tell them. He could come back after you go back home. What then?"

Zoey shook again, tears running down her face.

Alex rubbed her hair. "Come on. We need to get my parents."

"Okay."

He wiped her tears with the back of his hand, and then kissed both of her cheeks. "I'll be with you when you tell them."

She nodded again.

"It'll be okay. I'm sure he's gone by now."

"Let's get this over with."

He grabbed her hand and led the way to his parents' room.

Telling

ALEX WAS SURPRISED to see his mom and dad in the bed together. They were even snuggled against each other. He almost hated to disturb them, but the thought of an intruder in the house drove fear straight into his core, especially after what the man had done to Zoey. They needed to get the d-bag and throw him in jail.

"Mom! Dad! Wake up."

They both sat up, mumbling.

"Someone was in the house."

His dad stared at him. "What?"

"Zoey saw him."

"What? Are you okay?" his mom asked, looking at Zoey.

Alex squeezed her hand, and she went over the story again.

His dad jumped out of bed. "We need to call the cops. How did he even get in? I set the alarm before I went to bed. Did one of you turn it off?"

They both shook their heads.

Zoey started crying. "Do I have to tell the cops? I don't want to relive it again."

Alex's mom climbed out of bed and gave her a hug. "I'm so sorry that happened to you, Zoey. We promised your mom we'd keep you safe, and then this happened. We need to tell the police so they can catch him."

"Then we're changing all of our locks and codes. Lyss, you call them while I check everything out. You guys all stay in here." He put on a robe, grabbed a baseball bat, and left.

"I'm going to call the police. You two sit down. This might take a few minutes," said his mom.

They sat on the bed, Alex not letting go of Zoey's hand. His parents hadn't noticed their hand-holding, but then again, it was still dark. He could see his mom scrolling through numbers on her phone. "Officer Anderson? This is Alyssa Mercer. Our house was broken into…yes…no…okay. Thanks. Goodbye." She put the phone down, and looked over at Alex and Zoey. "They're going to come over and check things out. Probably the same ones who talked with us down at the station last night, since they've already been working with us."

"Should we go downstairs?" Alex asked. He squeezed Zoey's hand again. He could hear her sniffling, but he didn't dare wrap his arms around her like he wanted. Then again, maybe his mom wouldn't think anything of it under the circumstances.

"Let's wait for your dad to get back. We don't even know if the intruder is still here." She looked at Zoey. "How long ago did you see him?"

"I don't know. I was pretty cold when I woke up in the garage, so I had probably been there a while."

She gave Zoey another hug. "I'm so sorry. I feel horrible."

"It's not your fault."

Alex scooted closer to Zoey, and the three of them sat in silence until his dad returned. "No one's here now. I checked everywhere."

"What about the alarm? Was that still set? Is anything gone?"

"The alarm is set, and no, I didn't notice anything missing. Who knows what might have been taken? But running into Zoey could have distracted him enough to leave." He turned to Zoey. "You could be a hero in all of this."

"I might have given him some bruises, but I'm no hero."

"We're all safe, and you're the only one who saw him. I'd say you're a hero."

One thing Alex appreciated about his dad was that he was good at making people feel better when they were upset. He always found some angle that no one else would ever think of, and then cheered the person up. Alex let go of her hand and wrapped his arm around her. "I agree. You're braver than you think."

The doorbell rang. His parents ran out of the room. Alex helped Zoey up and gave her a kiss he'd been wanting to since they entered his parents' room. "It's going to be okay. Are you?"

She sighed and leaned her head against his. "I hope so. I don't know how much more I can take. Everything with Macy and now this."

He rubbed her back. "I know. How much are we supposed to put up with? Maybe after this, our parents won't make us go back to school."

Alex grabbed Zoey's hand, and they went downstairs. Zoey dropped his hand once the grown-ups were in sight. His parents were sitting in the living room with the same three cops from the night before.

The only two places left to sit were at the opposite ends of the room. He let Zoey pick one, and then he sat in the other. He kept his eyes on her, hoping that would express his support as she went over her story for the third time.

When she was done, Detective Fleshman turned to Alex. "Did you see or hear anything?"

He shook his head. "I was sleeping. I didn't hear anything until Zoey came and got me."

"What did she say?"

"Um, she said something about being glad I was okay."

"Then what?"

"Then I asked her what happened, and she told me exactly what she told you. Then I said we needed to tell my parents, so we did."

Officer Reynolds looked at Zoey. "Can you think of anything you left out? Anything, no matter how insignificant can help."

Zoey hesitated, but then shook her head.

"What is it?" asked Detective Fleshman.

"It's stupid." Zoey bit her lower lip.

"Let us be the judge."

Zoey looked at Alex and then back to the detective. "Well, he said I shouldn't be in Heather's room. But I was in Macy's room. Maybe he had the wrong house."

"Could be," said Anderson. "Or it could be important. Thank you for telling us." He scribbled on his notepad.

"Is there anything else, Zoey?" asked Reynolds.

Zoey shook her head.

The policemen were done asking questions and said they wanted to look around. When the room cleared out, Alex sat next to Zoey, wrapping his arm around her. "What's the deal with Heather?"

"I have no idea. I feel dumb even bringing it up."

"Maybe it'll be a major clue. You never know."

Tears filled her eyes. "Maybe. I just want to forget about it."

"I know. Me too."

Alyssa came back into the room. She started to say something, but then saw how upset Zoey was. She sat down next to her, wrapping her arm around her. "I can't apologize enough for what happened. Are you going to be okay?"

Zoey nodded. "I don't want to talk about it."

She kissed the top of Zoey's head. "We need to tell your mom about what happened."

"No." The tears spilled onto her face.

Alex felt helpless. He wanted to move his mom out of the way and comfort his girlfriend. "I can tell her what happened, Mom. Don't make Zoey go over it again. She's been through enough."

"You're so sweet, Alex. You've always been such a good friend to Zoey. Don't worry, I'll call Valerie in the morning and let her know what happened. Our house will be safer now. The police are going to have someone watch our house. That, and we're getting all the locks changed as soon as the stores open in the morning."

Alex glared at his mom. "She looks tired. Can we go to sleep now?"

"That's a good idea. Get some rest, you two."

The three of them went upstairs, Alyssa staying close to Zoey. She said goodnight to Alex in the hall and then followed Zoey into Macy's room. Alex watched as they went into the room, wanting to stay with Zoey, but knowing that would have to wait.

He went into his room, intending to wait until his mom went to bed so he could talk with Zoey, but as soon as he saw his bed he realized how tired he was. He climbed in, falling asleep almost immediately—the only benefit to all the crap in his life.

As he was dreaming of a reunion with Macy, something woke him. He felt a hand on his arm, but he knew that if he woke up, he would lose Macy. He fought to stay in his dream and be with his sister.

The hand shook him, and a voice whispered his name. In his dream, he hugged Macy, clinging to her. He begged her to stay, but knew the dream would vanish in a poof soon. With tears in his eyes, he begged to her come back home. "I need my big sister, Macy. I love you."

She vanished before his eyes and it took him a moment to realize that Zoey was sitting next to him.

Her eyes were wide. "I can't sleep. Not after running into that guy. I don't want to be alone. Can I sleep in here?"

Alex's heart raced. "Sure."

"Thanks." She climbed in while he scooted over.

A strange mixture of emotions ran through him. The desperation from wanting Macy back lingered, along with a lump in his throat, but at the same time nervousness and excitement ran through him having Zoey in there with him. "Are you okay?"

"Not really. I was so scared. I didn't know if that guy was going to kill me or what. I didn't want to end up missing too, so I fought harder than I thought I could. He still over-powered me, though." Her voice sounded unsteady.

Alex reached his arms around her. "You're safe now."

"I don't feel like it."

He felt a tear land on his arm. He scooted even closer to her, holding her tighter. "You are. I'm here and there are cops sitting out front. That dude would be stupid to come back."

Zoey rolled onto her back, rubbing her eyes. "Why did he leave me in the garage? I don't get it."

"I don't know, but I'm glad he did. I couldn't take it if something happened to you too."

"Do you think someone took Macy like that?" asked Zoey.

"She went willingly, right?" At least that's what Zoey kept telling him. "She's off with Jared, having the time of her life."

Zoey sighed, but didn't reply. She probably didn't believe it any more than he did. He had a feeling that she kept talking about Macy being with Jared so she didn't have to deal with the pain. She turned, looking at him. "Do you think she's okay?"

"She has to be. She's the most stubborn person I've ever met. If anyone can survive…something bad happening, it's her."

"I worry about her, you know?" Zoey said. "She never really stood up for herself against the bullies at school. She just hid inside herself. There were times she wouldn't even talk to me after those stupid jerks went off on her. She built such a high wall, keeping everyone out."

Alex played with a strand of her hair. "I know. Why do you think I kept teasing her? When we were kids, making her laugh always worked. She'd come right out of her shell. But it's more than a shell; she built a fortress around herself. If she wasn't letting either of us in, what was really going on?"

"Only Jared knows. I knew she told him more than she told me, but I never pushed it. I guess because I felt bad about keeping us a secret. I wish I had been there for her more. Maybe she would still be here." Zoey sniffled.

He sat up, forcing her to also. "Are you kidding me? I've never seen a better best friend. All of my life, you've been there for her."

"We drifted apart, Alex, and I did nothing about it. I went out practically every night instead of spending the night with her since she couldn't go anywhere."

"Don't blame yourself. She was shutting everyone out, like you said."

"I shouldn't have given up so easily! Don't you see that? If I would have come over more, maybe she would have opened up." Zoey wiped at her eyes again.

"There's plenty everyone could have done to change things. I could have stopped teasing her. Dad could have stopped being so critical. Both my parents could have given her more freedom. Neither one of them noticed that she was practically starving herself while she lost her weight. Dad was just mad about her refusing to eat meat. Those kids at school—don't even get me started. They're the ones to blame."

Zoey shook, not saying anything.

Alex pulled her close, listening to her breathe and took in her scent. He wanted to know what she was thinking, but figured it was best to give her space to think. She leaned her head against his, both of them silent.

Finally, she spoke. "I'm so scared, Alex. I don't want anything to happen to Macy and I don't ever want to see another intruder again. I want everything to go back to the way it was."

He held her tighter, hoping that showed his agreement. He wasn't used to seeing this side of her and wasn't sure how to react. Usually she was so tough, but that guy had really shaken her up—not that Alex blamed her.

She rolled over so that she was in his lap, and stared into his eyes. He moved some hair out of her face and kissed her lightly on the lips. She pushed herself against him, kissing him harder.

Alex was surprised, but he pulled her closer, returning the kiss. Unable to breathe, he ran his hands through her hair. After a moment, he sat back and looked at her. "Are you okay? Are we moving too fast?"

"No." She forced her lips on his again, this time opening his mouth with her lips.

His eyes opened wide with surprise. Was this really the time for this? His heart raced. Of course he would have loved to take things to another level, but were they really ready? She already had so many regrets with Macy's disappearance. He didn't want her to have more regrets—especially when it came to him.

She brought her tongue into his mouth and he jumped. They bumped noses.

"Ow." Zoey sat back, rubbing her nose. "I don't think that's supposed to happen."

He couldn't help smiling, and they both laughed.

She leaned back against the pillow. "Maybe now isn't the time for that. I think going to sleep in your arms would be nice enough."

"Me too." He put his arms around her again.

She ran her fingers along his arm, and he couldn't help flexing. She kept rubbing his arm, and then after a minute her arm fell to the bed. He could hear her breathing heavily.

"Sweet dreams." He kissed her hair and closed his own eyes.

Light

MACY FELT SOMETHING move along her hand. She didn't even bother trying to roll away. What was the point?

Part of her wanted to cry, but she couldn't. She had already cried and screamed more than she could bear. Her shoulders were in constant pain from having her wrists tied behind her back. Her legs were wet and cold from not being able to remove her pants to relieve herself. Even worse than that, the back of her legs burned with a relentless intensity. She could feel the sores back there from the dried excrement.

She had passed being hungry. Earlier, she had been so hungry she would have eaten rodents if she could have. Now she felt nothing in her stomach.

She was sure she had been down there for a few days, though she had no way of knowing for sure with cloth over her eyes. And even if it weren't for the blindfold, her thoughts were all over the place, and she was pretty sure she was going crazy.

Although the fact that she questioned her sanity gave her hope that she still held onto a shred of it.

Her throat was parched.

Chester had left her water before, but even if he had this time she had no way of getting it. She had rolled around the floor at one point, hoping to find some. It had been futile, and she had only made herself thirstier in the process.

Sounds of the trap door moving caught her attention. Was she actually hearing it? Or was this further proof of her slipping sanity?

Thud. That sounded like something landing on the floor above. *Squeak, squeak.* That sounded like the ladder. *Thump.* Two feet landing on the dirt floor. Was he going to rescue her?

"Are you ready to follow directions now, Heather?"

The voice sounded real, but so had the others.

"You have to be thirsty." She felt fingers tugging on the duct tape. In one solid, painful motion, the tape was ripped from her face. Then she felt tugging on the blindfold. Bright light blinded her. Macy closed her eyes as tight as she could and shoved her face into the dirt floor, trying to get away. After so long in the dark, it was too much. "You didn't answer my question. Are you ready to be good?"

She kept rolling around, trying to escape the light. Even though she closed her eyes, they refused to adjust.

"Your grandparents are going to be gone for a couple of hours, so now is the time to go back to the house and get cleaned up. Or I can leave you here longer. It's up to you."

"I'll go. Take me with you."

"Are you going to be good now? I need to know we won't have a repeat of the other night."

"Yes. Anything."

"Looks like we'll have to throw these clothes away. Or should I save them as a reminder in case you act up again?"

"No."

"Good. Let's get you up there so you'll be cleaned up when Grandma and Grandpa get back. I told them we took a road trip. You'll be able to go along with that story, right?"

Macy nodded.

"What? I can't hear you."

"Yes."

"And do you remember falling down the stairs?"

"What?"

"That's how you got all those bruises. Do you remember?"

"I remember."

A shadow blocked the sun as he moved behind her. There was a snip, followed by another. Her arms fell free to her sides and then her ankles spread apart from each other. Pain shot through her arms, and tears stung her eyes.

"Look at those marks. You'll need to wear long sleeves until they heal. Understand?"

Macy nodded, focused on how much she hurt everywhere.

"Stand up." Chester kicked her in the side.

Keeping her eyes closed, she pushed against the ground. Sharp pains ran through her arms. Her butt and legs stung where sores had formed. "I can't."

"There is no can't. Should I leave you here?"

"No!" She ignored the pain and forced herself to stand up.

"Open your eyes."

Macy's legs wobbled underneath her. What would he do to her if she fell? She swallowed and forced her eyes open. The light was even worse, but she couldn't risk him leaving her down there again. She blinked fast, trying to get her eyes to adjust.

"Are you thirsty?"

She nodded. The pain in her shoulders was too much. She pushed her arms behind her back, relieving some of it.

"There's some water in the house. Let's go."

Macy groaned. Could she even make it that far?

Chester went to the rope ladder and climbed up. He looked down at her. "Come on up."

She forced one foot in front of the other, stumbling with each step. Pins and needles ran through her legs, feeling the most painful at the bottom of her feet. The sores hurt even worse as she moved her legs.

The ladder was about six feet away. How was she going to make it there, much less to the farmhouse?

"Can you hurry up? We need to get you cleaned up before your grandparents get back."

She stumbled forward, forcing herself to go faster despite the various pains screaming out at her. Tears stung her eyes again, making her vision blurry. She managed to get to the ladder, but as soon as she brought her arms forward the pain became so intense that she jumped. She couldn't even bring them to her sides without it hurting. How was she supposed to pull herself up the ladder?

"What are you waiting for?"

"I can't."

"What is it with you? Are you an Ameri-can or an Ameri-can't?"

She stared at him, ignoring the pains in her neck. What kind of a stupid question was that?

"Get up here or I'll leave you down there until they leave again. I can't guarantee when that will be." He moved the door.

"No. I'll do it."

Macy held her breath, anticipating the pain. She moved her hands in front of her as fast as she could, hoping that would eliminate some of it. It didn't help. She would have to push through it.

Her grip was weak, but she managed to grab onto the ladder. She closed her eyes as the tears began to fall. Soon she would be getting out of the dirty clothes and getting cleaned up. That's what she had to focus on; otherwise the pain would be too much. Beads of sweat formed around her face.

She cried the whole way up, but she made it, thinking of the bathtub and new clothes. Maybe she could put some ointment on the sores on her legs. They were probably infected since she hadn't been able to clean them. Each sore felt hot, and it got even worse every time her pants rubbed against her legs.

When she reached the top, she wasn't able to pull herself up onto the floor. Everything hurt, and she didn't have the strength. She had barely made it to the top of the ladder. What if she fell to the ground below?

"Help me. I ca…I need help."

He stared at her.

"Please," she begged.

"Oh, all right. Since you asked nice." He reached down and grabbed her arm, roughly, and yanked her up.

She fell to the floor, rubbing her arm where he had grabbed her.

"Get up. They're going to be back soon. You need to get cleaned up, and I have to get rid of this beard. I've gone too long without shaving."

Groaning, she forced herself back up again. He slammed the trap door shut and kicked some hay over it.

"Let's get to the house." He walked on ahead of her. Did he expect her to keep up?

She forced herself to walk. Her muscles ached, and the sores burned, but at least the pins and needles had gone away. That was something at least. Her arms naturally went behind her back, relieving the pain. She would have to hold them forward once George and Ingrid came back, but for now, she was going to nurse her wounds.

He turned around and waited once he got to the barn door. "Hurry up."

"I'm going as fast as I can."

"You can do better than that. Oh, by the way, I saw your old family."

Macy stopped. She stared at him, her many questions not reaching her mouth.

"They were all sleeping when I got there, so I let myself in. Your best friend was in your room. She wasn't sleeping, and that threw me off. I had to shut her up."

The blood drained from her body. "What did you do?"

"Oh, she's fine. She woke up cold, but otherwise unharmed. I couldn't let her wake anyone else. Pick up your pace, and I'll tell you more."

Her heart raced. What had he done? Was Zoey okay? What about her parents and Alex? She walked faster, ignoring the searing pain. "What did you do?" she asked again.

He walked through the door, waited for her to exit, and then he closed the barn door. "First, I got rid of your bloody clothes. Your old family was pretty upset about seeing them." He turned to look at her. "They probably already think you're dead. That's the plan. They're going to move on, so you don't need to worry about those ties anymore. You're Heather, and I'm your dad. Don't forget that."

She nodded. Her family wouldn't move on. They wouldn't. Or would they?

"Oh, and keep in mind that I got back in again. I didn't hurt anyone…this time. Don't get mouthy with me again, or I won't be so nice next time."

Her sores burned as she walked. He thought this was nice? Why had he gone into her house again? Just to threaten her? Had he actually done anything to her family? He admitted to doing something to Zoey, but supposedly she was okay. What exactly did he consider "okay?" He probably thought Macy was okay, but she needed to have a doctor look at the sores. She knew that would never happen.

When they finally got to the house, he opened the door for her. "Why don't you go to your room and grab some clean clothes? Then you can get a bath. I'll shave in my room—don't worry about me."

As if she would. She nodded and walked past him.

"Wait."

She stopped.

"Give your ol' dad a hug."

Was he serious?

He opened his arms. Apparently he was. "Come on, Heather. I've missed your hugs. Throw your dad a bone."

Macy caught a glance of the barn through a window. She didn't ever want to go back there again. She stifled a gag and walked to him. He wrapped his arms around her.

"That's not a hug, Heather. Give me a real hug."

Gritting her teeth, she wrapped her arms around him, ignoring the pain, and gave a little squeeze. Even more pain shot through her arms.

He hugged her tighter. "That's my girl. Now go get cleaned up. We're going to have a great time with your grandparents when they get back."

Macy walked back to the room that was supposed to be hers. It was Heather's, and always would be. When she walked through the door she froze, her heart skipping a beat. Her favorite teddy bear from her real bedroom was sitting on the bed.

He really had been back to her house. Chills ran down her back. Even so, she ran to the bed and scooped up the bear, hugging it tight, not caring about how much her arms hurt. It was something familiar, something loved.

The smell of her home, her *real* home, brought instant comfort. She squeezed the stuffed animal all the tighter, pretending that she was back home and that she had never sneaked out to meet Jared.

She threw herself onto the bed, careful not to hurt her sores, imagining that she was back on her own bed. Macy buried her face into the bear's stomach and breathed in the smells even harder. She could see her room in her mind—every detail.

Would the bear hold the scent forever? Could she go back home in her mind whenever she wanted now?

A pounding on the door brought her back to reality. "Are you going to get in the bathroom? Your grandparents are going to be back soon," called Chester.

"Coming!" She squeezed the stuffed animal, never wanting to let go.

Hardware

CHAD FELT DIZZY looking at all the choices for door locks. Wasn't a lock just a lock? The aisle was full of different types. Not wanting to read another box, he grabbed five boxes of the most expensive lock on the shelf. It had to be the best or it wouldn't cost so much.

Just as he set the last one in the basket, his phone rang. It was Alyssa.

"Is everything okay?"

"Just wanted to let you know that someone from the home security will be here in a couple hours. They're going to look at everything and make sure nothing is faulty. If it is, they'll upgrade us for free."

"They're going to upgrade us, period. I'll be there before they arrive. I've got the locks. Do you need me to get anything else?"

"No. There's a police car out front, so if there's any trouble, they're here."

"Good. I told them not to leave while I was gone. I'll be home soon."

"Okay. Chad?"

"Yeah?"

"I love you."

His heart swelled up. "I love you too, Lyss. Stay safe."

"Okay."

The call ended and he stuffed the phone back in his pocket. It was so nice to be getting along again, and he had been surprised at how quickly his old feelings had returned. He found himself eager to get back home to her. He picked up the basket and headed for the registers.

He had to turn down another aisle to get there. As he did, he saw Lydia. What was she doing in the hardware store? Had she been following him?

Chad turned around, but it was too late.

She ran to him. "What are you doing here?" she asked.

"I was about to ask you the same thing. You're not following me, are you?"

Lydia's face fell. "I thought we were close."

"Look, Lydia, you're a really sweet person—"

"Oh, geez. I can tell where this is going."

"I appreciate you being there for me when I was going through a tough time, but I need to focus on my family now."

"Right. That's why I've been giving you space."

"Space? You're making my family dinner tonight."

"Do you want to explain to Alyssa why you don't want me over?"

Chad narrowed his eyes. "You know the answer to that."

"Then let me come over and cook you guys a meal. Everyone wants to help out. I called all the members of the homeowners' association, and each one signed up for a night to cook or bring you takeout. Everyone. Besides, I know how much you love my lasagna. I'll make it and leave. I don't have any ulterior motives. Well, maybe one."

"What?"

"Just to let you know that I'll be waiting. I'm not going anywhere, Chad. When you're ready, which I know you will be eventually, you can find me. I'll drop anything to spend time with you. I appreciate everything you do. Your blog is amazing. I know you'll be able to quit your day job any day now. And even though I doubt you've worked out lately, you still look hot as—"

"Okay, Lydia. Point taken. Why don't you try to rekindle things with Dean?"

She gave him an exasperated look. "The man who comes home three nights a month? No. You know why I stay with him: so I don't have to work. He works so much, I don't have to. Sure, I may have to fix a sprinkler head once in a while"—she held one up—"but other than that, I have the perfect life. Well, when you come over to play, I do."

Chad ran his free hand through his hair. "I need to get back home."

Lydia looked in his basket. "New locks? What's going on?"

"Why don't you ask Alyssa about it tonight? It'll give you something to talk about. Either that, or watch the news. Everything we do seems to end up there. I can't wait for the media to find someone else to stalk."

She raised an eyebrow. "I hope everything is okay. I'll see you tonight."

He nodded and turned to walk away. Why was she everywhere? He needed to get her out of his life so he could focus on Alyssa. She was the one he loved. Lydia had been nothing more than a distraction when Alyssa wouldn't give him the time of day. Lydia was a mistake, and one that he intended to forget about.

When he got to the register, the girl behind the counter stared at him.

"Are you all right?" he asked.

"You're…you're the guy from the news."

He nodded. "I need to buy these."

"Oh, right. Sorry." She grabbed the basket and scanned the first box. "I'm so sorry about your daughter. She's beautiful, by the way. I hope she's okay."

Chad squirmed. This was why he hated going anywhere any more. It had been this way since Macy disappeared.

"Are you changing your locks?"

"Um, yeah."

"Aren't you afraid that if she tries to get in, she won't be able to? Won't she feel like you're trying to lock her out?"

Anger burned inside of him. "Not that it's any of your business, but our house is a target. If Macy comes back, she has the smarts to knock or use the doorbell."

A manager walked up to them. "Is everything all right here?"

Chad turned to him. "I'm trying to buy some locks to keep my family safe, and your cashier is trying to give me a guilt trip about my daughter."

The manager stared at him for a moment. Then recognition covered his face. "Oh, Mr. Mercer. We're honored to have your patronage. Please accept my apologies. This is my daughter, Sarah, and her mouth gets out of control when she's nervous. Let me give you those locks at a discount. Does fifty percent sound good?"

"I'm not looking for a discount. I want to get home and get these locks in without having to explain myself to anyone." He was aware of people staring, but he really didn't care.

"Seventy-five percent off. Now that's a deal, and those are our best locks. Houdini himself couldn't get through a door with those."

Chad shook his head. He pulled out his wallet, counted out the cash, and put them on the counter. "Keep the change." He stormed out of the store, never more eager to get back home. He was going to have to find a new hardware store.

He was glad to have the job of replacing all the door locks when he got home. He needed the distraction. But it didn't work; he kept hearing the voice of the cashier saying he was locking Macy out. By the third door, he couldn't take it anymore. He threw his tools down, swearing.

Chad needed his dad. He would know what to do. In fact, his parents would have flown in the moment they heard Macy was gone. He tried to picture his dad standing next to him. It was useless. His imagination wouldn't bring his parents back any more than it was going to bring back his daughter.

He leaned against the door and slid to the ground, staring into the back yard. Tears filled his eyes, blurring his vision. What was he supposed to do? He wanted to keep the locks that Macy could use, but at the same time he *had* to protect his family. Someone had gotten into their house while they all slept. He had no other choice. Macy would understand.

She loved them all and wanted them safe. Just as he loved her and wanted her safe.

But there was nothing he could do to protect her. He hated feeling helpless, and this was the worst kind of helpless.

Sure, he was the kind of dad who would tell his kids to toughen up when they got a scrape, but it wasn't that he didn't care. He just wanted them to be able to handle life.

He sighed, more tears welling up in his eyes, threatening to spill out.

Did Macy need him as much as he needed his parents right now? He rested his head on his knees, shaking with sobs.

This was the worst part: not being able to do anything. At least with the doors, he could do something useful. He was protecting his family. But that cashier had planted doubts in his head about even that.

Screw her. He stood up and grabbed his tools. Screw that cashier.

What did she know, anyway? Did she have a missing kid? Was her family in danger? Screw her. She was probably one of those snot-nosed employees who ran to her dad whenever she had a problem.

He worked on getting the doorknob off so he could remove the lock. His vision was still blurry and now his hands were shaking. Why had he gone to that hardware store in the first place? He wouldn't make that mistake again, and he had every intention of writing all about it in his blog.

But Chad knew better than to write while he was upset. He didn't want to say anything that would hurt his reputation. If he came off as a jerk, that could potentially ruin how well his blog was going, or even worse, piss people off who were looking for Macy. He needed to keep the public's sympathy.

"Are you okay?" came Alyssa's voice from the other side of the door.

"Yeah," he lied.

"Can I come out?"

Chad wiped his face dry. "Sure."

She opened the knobless door and froze when she saw him. "What's the matter?"

"What do you think?"

"You don't need to snap at me."

"You're right. I'm sorry." He told her what had happened with the cashier, breaking down halfway through.

Alyssa's face softened. "Oh, Chad." She gave him a hug, and they stood in the back yard holding each other. "You know, you don't have to hide when you're hurting. I know you always want to talk with your dad, but I'm here. You can talk to me. This is something we're going through together."

"Do you think she'll understand?"

"Macy? Yes. She would want you doing exactly this. She would want us to be safe and to keep Alex protected."

"Why are we talking like she's dead? She *would* say this or that."

"Not because we think she's dead." Tears filled Alyssa's eyes. "Only because she's not here and we can't ask her."

He shook his head. "We're talking like she's dead."

News

CHAD STARED AT the computer screen, unable to focus. Lydia was in the kitchen, preparing the lasagna—because she knew how much he liked it. Why was she even in their house? Why hadn't he been able to stand up and tell her no?

Because that would have looked suspicious, and the last thing he needed was for Alyssa to figure out what he had done. It didn't matter now, because it was over. He wasn't going to see Lydia anymore. He was going to repair his marriage and find a way to get his daughter back.

The screen saver popped up, startling him. He leaned back in the chair, rubbing his hands over his stubble. He had to find a way to get Lydia out of his life. At least she lived at the other end of the neighborhood. It wasn't as though she was next door. He could avoid her easily enough. She would find another guy to keep her distracted from thinking about her own husband.

He got up and paced around the office, picking up stray items. The office was a mess. He hated how he let it get so messy in there, but when he was in there, he was focused on the computer. After what seemed like only a few minutes, his office was organized. Alyssa had always complained about the mess, but she hadn't said a word about it since Macy had been missing.

Where *was* Macy? He picked up a stack of business cards and threw it across the office, sending cards everywhere. What would he do if she never returned? There he went again, allowing himself to think about her being dead. That was the last thing he wanted, but he couldn't seem to keep his mind from going there. The more time that went by, the harder it became to keep his hope alive. It had only been a week. What would he be like in another week if Macy was still gone? How would he survive another week? He needed her back.

Chad picked up a pen from his desk and chucked it at a bookshelf. Distress rising in him, he picked up the coffee mug holding all of his pens and pencils. He squeezed it and then threw it at the wall above the couch. It burst into tiny pieces all over the cushions and floor.

It felt good to break something. He went over to the bookshelf and grabbed a handful of paperbacks, throwing them one by one across the room. Once he had thrown them all, he picked up all his knick-knacks and threw them at the couch, knowing that if they broke he would later regret it.

With the shelf empty, he went over to the couch and grabbed a throw pillow, shaking the broken mug pieces onto the floor. He put his face into the pillow and screamed as loud as he could until his throat hurt. No need for his family or Lydia to hear him.

The cell phone rang. He stared at it on his desk. A feeling of dread ran through him. What if it was bad news? He picked it up and recognized the police station number. How sad that he recognized that number now.

"Chad here."

"Mr. Mercer, this is Officer Anderson. We need you and your wife to come down to the station."

"Again? Why?" Chad demanded.

"We need you two to come alone."

His blood ran cold. Had they found Macy? "Tell me what this is about."

"Sir, we received the results from the clothes."

"What? You said it could be a week or more."

"With this being such a high profile case, they rushed it to the front."

"Why do you need us to go back downtown? Can't you tell me over the phone? My family has been through enough, wouldn't you agree?"

"I can't deny that, but it's policy."

"You think I care about policies? If you have something important to tell us, either tell us over the phone or drive over here yourselves."

"Mr. Mercer, please. We—"

"I'm not dragging my wife back down there. After what happened last night, I'm sure as hell not leaving the house without my son. He's only thirteen. After everything we've gone through, he'll be lucky if we ever leave him alone again."

There was a sigh on the other end of the line. "If you really want us to come to your house, I'll talk with my supervisor. I'll see if we can make an exception."

"I think you probably can." Chad hung up before he said something he would regret. He stuck the phone in his pocket and went upstairs to find Alyssa. When he passed the kitchen, he saw her talking with Lydia.

His stomach twisted in knots. Lydia wouldn't tell Alyssa anything, would she? No. She wouldn't want word to get back to Dean.

Chad looked at Alyssa. "I need to talk to you for a moment."

A look of fear washed over her face. "What's going on? I don't like your tone."

"I got a call from the station."

She got up and grabbed his arm, dragging him up the stairs toward their bedroom. "What do they want? What's going on?"

"They got the results on the blood."

Alyssa stopped. She stared at Chad expectantly.

"I don't know, though I'm assuming it's Macy's. They wouldn't tell me over the phone. Anderson wanted us to go down to the station, but I told him that wasn't going to happen, so they're going to come here."

She leaned against the wall. "Do you really think it's her blood?"

"Who else would it belong to? Those were her clothes, right? If it was someone else's they would have told me over the phone, don't you think?"

"What are we going to do?"

"Keep looking. Keep hoping. It's like I said before: sure it was a lot of blood, but it wasn't enough to k…to do any real damage. I've bled more than that when I've been punched in the nose. Obviously, the clothes were removed because they needed to be replaced. The cops found them by the mall, so she probably bought some new clothes, put them on, and dropped those. This is actually good news."

Alyssa looked at him as though he had lost his mind.

"I'm serious. It means she's probably alive, and not too far away. The clothes weren't found right after she disappeared. It was about a week later. So she has to be nearby." Maybe if he kept talking, he would start to believe the crap coming out of his mouth. "It means we have to canvas the neighborhood even more. Maybe we should even accept an invitation to speak to the press again. We need all the public sympathy we can get. If people hear from us directly, you know, the ones who haven't visited my blog to hear from us there, maybe they'll help us look harder."

She looked a little bit more convinced than she had before.

"You know I'm right, Lyss. Once word gets out about this, people are going to want to hear more. It's the perfect time for us to get in front of the cameras and beg for people to help us find Macy."

"I think you're right."

Chad gave her a double-take. "What?"

"I know. You think you'll never hear that again, but you're right. This is probably good news. It gives us hope. She's probably not too far away. Maybe she'll even see the news. If she's hiding somewhere, mad at us for something, maybe seeing us on TV will be enough to bring our baby home."

He nodded, trying not to seem surprised that she had bought his load of horse manure.

"This is actually a good thing. My parents are still planning on coming Monday, so they'll be able to help us out. This is perfect. Everything is coming together."

"All we need is Macy."

Alyssa sighed. "That's all we need. Maybe if us speaking to the cameras isn't enough to bring her home, maybe my parents would do it."

"That's good. Should we tell Alex what's going on? He should know."

Alyssa nodded. "He should."

Chad rubbed his eyes. He wasn't used to Alyssa agreeing with him so much. He went to Alex's door and knocked. He could hear a noise behind the door. It sounded like something heavy falling onto the ground, followed by some rustling noises. "You in there, Alex?"

"Yeah. Come in."

He opened the door. Alex was sitting up in his bed, not wearing a shirt. "Where's your shirt and why are you sweaty?"

"I'm tired. I haven't slept in, like, a week. This is how I sleep now.

What's with all the questions?"

There was a rustling noise at the other end of the bedroom.

"What was that?" Chad asked.

"Uh…um, I was playing with Macy's ferret. Yeah, that's it. He looked lonely."

Chad raised an eyebrow. "Don't let that thing get lost. Anyway, the police are on their way over with news about Macy's clothes. Did you want to be there to hear it? They didn't think you should be, but Mom and I wanted to ask you what you want. She's your sister, and if you want to hear the news when we do, you can."

The color drained from his face. "Is it going to be bad?"

"We don't know. But Mom and I think even if it is Macy's blood, it's good news." He repeated his stupid theory to Alex, who also seemed to buy it. "So, we'll see you downstairs?"

Alex nodded.

Alyssa moved next to Chad. "Well, we'd better tell Zoey. She'll probably want to be there, too."

"No!" Color drained from Alex's face. "I mean, I'll tell her. You guys do…whatever it is you have to do. I'll get her and then we'll meet you guys downstairs."

Chad raised an eyebrow. "All right. We'll see you guys down there. Don't forget to put the ferret back in the cage."

Alex sighed. "Yeah, okay."

Chad closed the door and walked downstairs with Alyssa.

Despite everything, the smell of the lasagna made his mouth water. He wasn't sure what Lydia put into it, but hers was the best there was.

"Do you think Alex was acting strange?" Alyssa asked.

"He's thirteen. I'd be more worried if he wasn't acting weird."

"I suppose. Well, I'll let Lydia know what's going on. I'm not sure how much time is left until the food's ready, but it smells so good, it must be close."

Chad nodded. He went into the living room and saw the police cruiser pull up across the street. Now there were two cop cars sitting in front of their house. He stuffed his tools in a corner behind a chair and then opened the front door before they even had a chance to knock.

Chad exchanged greetings with the police, and they all sat down in the living room. Alyssa joined them, and Alex came down with Zoey a minute later.

The news had been what they all expected. The blood was Macy's, and even the cops agreed it wasn't a fatal amount. There was still plenty of reason to keep hope alive.

Even so, it felt like someone had punched Chad in the side of the head. He had known those would be the results, but hearing it out loud brought the truth to a whole new level. He looked over at Alyssa, who was staring out the window with tears shining in her eyes. He put his arm around her and pulled her close.

She started sobbing, shaking almost violently in his arms. "We'll find her," he whispered. "This is good news, remember?" He wasn't sure if he bought it any more than he had earlier, but he had to hold onto the hope that she was still alive. He had to.

Crushed

MACY BARELY HAD enough time to get ready before Chester's parents returned. They kept her busy walking around the farm, having her help with the chores. Every move she made hurt; she couldn't walk without the sores rubbing against her clothes.

She smiled through the pain so they wouldn't know anything was wrong. One wrong move, and she would go back into the dungeon. She might not get out if there was a next time.

The sores were so painful she had no chance of a getaway. Her joints still ached from being forced into one position for days. Even if she didn't have to worry about Chester running after her, it would hurt too much to get far.

After pouring some feed for the pigs, Macy sat down to rest. Tears stung at her eyes. She forced a smile. That's what Heather would do.

Ingrid walked by a minute later and stopped. "Heather, why does your dad insist on so many road trips? Three days this time. What did you two do for three days?" Ingrid patted Macy's shoulders. "And how did you manage to fall down two flights of stairs? Those bruises look so painful."

"Just clumsy, I guess."

Ingrid shook her head. "I'm sure you were distracted. I can't imagine how hard everything is for you. What with your mom being gone, he shouldn't drag you around, forcing you to stay in a car for days on end."

Macy looked into her eyes. She opened her mouth to say she wasn't Heather, but images of the cellar flooded her mind. She just shrugged.

George came over. "Tired? Poor girl. Does being around the animals help? It always did when you were little."

"Yeah, sure."

"We should tell Chester to take a road trip on his own," Ingrid said. "We can watch Heather. It would do her a world of good, especially since she has to deal with the divorce. It's too much."

"You know how he is," George said. "Remember that one kid picked on him every day?"

Macy looked up, suddenly interested.

"Juan, wasn't it?" Ingrid asked. "He was always envious of Chester."

"I don't know about that, but they were always fighting," George said. "Seems Chester came home beat up nearly every day for a while, but he just kept going back to school. When times are tough, he won't let anything stop him. Now he's forcing Heather to push through."

"He's a stubborn one. Seems those teachers should have done more for him." Ingrid shook her head. "They were old-school, even for that time. Boys will be boys, they told me every time I complained."

"The teachers practically encouraged the other kids to make fun of him. That's what Chester always said."

Ingrid patted Macy's arm. "We're upsetting Heather. Let's talk about something more cheery. Would you like your dad to take a vacation while you stay here?"

Macy's eyes lit up. "Yes, please."

George picked up a pitchfork that was lying on the ground and leaned against the wall. "I should convince him to go back to Paris. He needs to try harder to get Karla back. Heather is her life. Why would she throw everything away? And why wouldn't Chester fight for her?"

Ingrid cleared her throat. "We ought to let Heather get some rest."

When Macy finally made it to her bedroom, she was so tired that she climbed into bed without putting on pajamas.

Aside from being physically wiped out, she was mentally tired from pretending to be someone else. But the last thing she wanted was to go back to the horrible room under the barn again, so she kept up the facade. Spending time with the animals in the barn was a painful reminder of where she would go again if she didn't do exactly what Chester wanted.

Her mom was off in Paris, sowing her wild oats. Her dad was the deranged lunatic who had nearly left her to die just to prove a point. The kind elderly couple were her grandparents. The farm was her home, and she had no friends aside from the animals. This was her life.

When she looked into the eyes of the animals, they almost seemed to know that she was unhappy. She could plaster on a smile for George and Ingrid, but there was no fooling the large, brown eyes of the cows and horses. When she was near them, they stared at her as though staring into the depths of her soul. Macy had felt understood each time she made eye contact with them. They knew her secret somehow, and they were going to keep it safe.

She moved aside the pillow to pick up her teddy, but it wasn't where she had left it. Dread washed over her. Even though she was fifteen, she needed that bear. She had slept the previous night with it in her face the whole time.

Macy picked up the pillow, lifting it over her head. Nothing. She put it back and looked around on the floor. It could have fallen off, even though she had been careful to leave it right next to the pillow that morning. She wanted to keep it safe, comfortable even. Obviously, it was a toy, but it was more than that.

Not caring about her sores, she crawled around on the floor, looking for where the bear could have gone. It wasn't under the bed or the dresser. It was nowhere.

She had to get it. She picked up the covers from the perfectly made bed. Chester made her keep the room pristine, so she would have seen a lump if it was there, but she had to look anyway. She moved to the closet, searching for it in there.

After she had looked everywhere three times, she threw herself onto the bed and sobbed into the pillow. It was gone. Chester had to have taken it. Was it another cruel way for him to control her? Had he given it to her just to give her hope so that he could take it away, crushing her yet again? Trying to confuse her as to her own identity?

Could he be any worse? He wanted her to accept him as her dad, yet he acted like the world's biggest jerk. Hadn't he ever heard of winning people over by being nice?

Her stomach ached by the time she was done crying. She had nothing left in her. Macy felt like an empty shell of a person. Was that the point? Was that exactly what Chester wanted? If that was the case, he had won.

Her heart felt as though it had been ripped to shreds.

She got up and turned the light off. She climbed into bed alone, with no stuffed animal to hold. Even though she was exhausted, she couldn't sleep.

The way he talked about himself, one would think he was a hero, saving her from her life with her real family.

She couldn't see an end in sight. Would he let her go to school? She had already missed however much time she had been gone. Why didn't his parents question it? If he sent her to school, she would at least get some time away from him and maybe make some friends. That was probably the exact thing he didn't want her to do.

She sniffed, needing to blow her nose. She couldn't recall seeing any tissues in the bedroom, so she would have to go to the bathroom to get some toilet paper. Maybe Chester had even put the bear in the hall as a mean reminder that she needed to stay in the room, just as he had done with the picture of her family. Macy hadn't seen that since the first night in the house.

She got out of bed and went to the door. She turned the knob, but her hand slid off. She tried again, but found it wouldn't move. He had locked her inside.

What if she had to use the bathroom? Hadn't he thought of that? She grabbed the knob and twisted it with all the force she could muster. It didn't move. She tried several more times before giving up.

Fresh tears poured down her face, and then she walked back over to the bed. Never before had she felt so dejected—and that was saying something after everything she had already been through.

She had no more fight left in her. She already knew the windows were bolted shut, so there was no way she was going to get out. Luckily she didn't have to go to the bathroom.

Pulling the covers up to her chin, she closed her eyes as the tears stopped. What was the point? What was crying going to get her? Macy found it too easy to push each and every thought out of her head. There was no point, was there? She couldn't get to her parents anyway. She didn't even know where she was, but Chester did. He had already gone back to her house, and the bear had been proof of that.

Had that been his real angle? To remind her that he could hurt them if he needed to? Would he really kill them all if she escaped? She wouldn't put it past him. He was cruel enough to put her through everything he had. It wouldn't take much more effort to finish someone off.

He didn't care about them. The people she loved the most meant nothing to him. He wouldn't even flinch at killing them. She was sure of it. If she were to get away, he would climb into his truck, drive back to her house, and kill them off before she could even figure out where she was, much less find a way to get back to them.

That was what the bear was all about. Just like with the picture, it was left for her to find it, and then it was gone. He wouldn't leave anything from her house long enough for her to hold onto.

But the memories were something he couldn't take from her. He could take everything else, and he pretty much already had, but he couldn't control her mind. She had every memory of her parents, friends, brother, house, and pets. He couldn't make her forget, even if he could make her call him dad. He would never *be* her dad.

Bar

ALYSSA SAT UP in bed, gasping for air. She was drenched in sweat, and her heart was racing. She had just had another nightmare about Macy. She had always had bad dreams about things happening to her kids, but since Macy had disappeared, waking up didn't help.

She wiped some wet strands of hair away from her face and looked over at Chad. He was sleeping, not snoring as usual, which meant he probably wasn't sleeping well either. When he was deep in sleep, he snored like a chainsaw.

Not wanting to have another bad dream, she got into the shower to get cleaned up. The images from her nightmare wouldn't leave. What made the nightmares worse was the fact that she had nothing good to focus on. When the kids were little, she would sneak into their rooms and watch them sleep peacefully. Even as they got older she did it on occasion, depending on how bad the dream was.

She couldn't do that now.

Physically, she was wiped out. Her legs ached and her neck and shoulders were sore. Had it not been for her racing mind, she could have crawled back into bed and slept for a day, if not more.

She couldn't stop thinking about the worst. Though she couldn't bring herself to say it out loud, she feared Macy's death. She knew that the longer she was gone, the higher the chances were of that happening. The thought of that made her want to vomit. No one had the right to take *her* child. No one. How dare they?

It just wasn't like Macy to take off like that. Even if she had planned on running away, she wouldn't have stayed away this long, causing all this mental anguish to her family. One time when she had been mad about not being allowed to go somewhere with her friends, Macy had staged her own personal hunger strike. That was her type of thing, not running away without a word.

Even if she had met someone online, she wouldn't have left like that. She just wouldn't have. As a mom, Alyssa knew these things. She wondered if her dreams were Macy calling out to her. Tears ran down her face, as they did so many times these days.

She cried until the water ran cold, and then she got dressed. There was no way she could stay in the house for another moment. After that last dream, too bloody to leave her mind, she couldn't sit still. Her home felt like it was closing in on her.

Chad stirred in the bed, startling her. He rolled over, letting out one short snore.

She sighed in relief. Normally, she would have hoped he would wake so she could talk about the dream. He was so good at calming her down, but she didn't want to be calmed down.

Hopefully getting out of the house would help. She grabbed her keys from the nightstand and headed for her car. It started up easily, despite the cold and its recent lack of use.

Alyssa didn't care where she went. She just needed a change of scenery. At least the roads were clear at this hour. She was able to just drive. Having something new to look at was nice, but it didn't change anything. Macy was still gone, and there was nothing she could do about it.

Her life was still spinning out of control. It would never stop until she had Macy back.

Before she knew it, she was at the other side of town. Chad always wanted to avoid the area, because it wasn't as safe as their neighborhood. Run-down apartment buildings lined the streets. There were far too many people on the sidewalks for that time of night. She was pretty sure she saw a drug deal go down at the trunk of a dilapidated old car.

Chills ran down her back. She hoped Macy wasn't here. She wouldn't come here on her own, would she? As Alyssa drove she scanned the people, hoping to see her daughter. Even though she couldn't stand the thought of Macy with the people she saw, she just wanted to see her baby, snatch her up and bring her home.

Not only would she have Macy back, but she would be a hero. She would be the one who found her daughter. Not that she really cared about fame, but after all the accusations, mostly in the media, it would be nice to shove it in everyone's face, letting them know she had absolutely nothing to do with whatever had happened to Macy.

After a few minutes, she was out of that part of town. In fact, she was out of their town and into the next one. It didn't look much different. There was still questionable activity on the streets, but she knew if she kept going she would hit the nicer part of the town. Eventually things became cleaner. There was a cute park, followed by some restaurants, and then a mall. Everything was closed.

A little beyond the mall sat a bar. Bright lights shone from inside, and the parking lot was nearly full. Her stomach rumbled. Maybe she could grab an appetizer and distract herself with whatever was going on inside. She flipped her blinker on and pulled into the parking lot, taking the first available spot she came across.

She checked her purse for cash, finding plenty. She could have a full meal and then some drinks, and still have money to spare. She didn't want to use the credit card and have to explain this to Chad later. She planned on getting back home before he woke up.

Even if he did wake up to find her gone, he wouldn't be able to blame her for needing to get out and see some new sights. It wouldn't fix anything, but maybe she could feel a little better for a short time. She grabbed a pink baseball cap and slid it on, hoping to avoid being recognized. Her family's images were all over the place.

She locked the car and headed inside. She could hear music and billiard balls clacking before she even reached the building.

When she stepped in, no one even glanced up at her. She saw an empty table near the back and took it. After she made herself comfortable, she watched everyone. A couple of rowdy games of pool went on at the far end of the bar. There were several TV's on the walls, all playing different channels. Music played from somewhere. It sounded like the music her kids listened to.

Her stomach rumbled, and she wondered if she was supposed to go up to the bar and order. She hadn't been to a bar in years, since before she was a parent.

Just as she was getting ready to get up, a waitress showed up in front of her. "What do you want?" She was chewing a big wad of gum. At least Alyssa hoped it was gum since she was serving food and drinks.

"Can I get something to eat?"

"Yeah." She pulled out a menu, handing it to Alyssa. "Anything to drink while you wait?"

"Do you have any specials?"

She nodded. "We have a good deal on a daiquiri in a fish bowl."

Alyssa looked around, noticing several others around the bar drinking from a fish bowl. She hoped there had never been fish in them. "I'll take one."

"Coming right up." She walked off, writing on her pad of paper.

It was nice to be treated like a normal human being for a change. For the last week, everyone had been treating her like a fragile doll—one wrong move and she would break.

She looked through the menu, her stomach growling hard. Why was she so hungry? She had eaten a lot of lasagna for dinner, despite being upset over the news about the blood. Maybe her body was trying to make up for lost meals. Didn't it know that the baby it had created was missing? Meals really didn't matter anymore.

The waitress came by, carrying a red fishbowl. She set it on the table in front of Alyssa. "What are you going to order?"

Alyssa ordered a plate of nachos and took a long drink from the straw, enjoying the warm sensations running through her as the liquid made its way to her empty stomach.

Her phone rang in her purse. Had Chad woken up? Grumbling, she pulled it out. It was Valerie. She was on the other end of the globe, and they had been playing phone tag since Zoey's encounter with the intruder. She was feeling more relaxed by the minute. She could handle the conversation now.

"Valerie. How are you?"

"Why is it so loud, Alyssa? Isn't it midnight over there?"

"Something like that. I couldn't sleep, so I put on a movie." Alyssa took another long sip. The fish bowl was half-empty, or was it half-full?

"Oh, okay. Well, what's going on? You sounded upset when you left the message yesterday. Although, you have every reason to be upset. I was just worried about Zoey. Is everything all right?"

"There was a little incident, but she's fine."

"What do you mean?"

It didn't feel like a big deal anymore. "Someone broke in our house, but we changed the locks and had the security system upgraded, so now everything is safer than ever. No one's getting back in." She took another drink.

"Is Zoey okay? Are all of you okay?"

"We're all fine. I didn't want to worry you, Valerie. She can tell you about it herself. She actually saw the guy—she was a hero. You should be proud. Because of her, they were able to draw a sketch of him. He looked like the unabomber, but they caught that guy, right?"

"Zoey saw him?"

"Yeah. She even tried to fight him off. Like I said, you should be proud of her. You raised a fine one, Valerie. Then she came and got us. She was upset, of course, but she didn't even want us to tell you what happened. We couldn't do that."

"She fought him off? Oh, dear lord. I've got to get back home."

"No. Don't do that. You've got all that work to catch up on. She's never been safer than she is now. At least at our house. No one is getting in or out without our knowledge. We got the most expensive of everything."

"Are you sure? I don't want to put any added pressure on you guys."

"No. Not at all. It's nice to have her with us. She and Alex are helping each other out. They've always been like siblings, and now they're really pulling together. It's cute actually."

"If you're sure."

"I can have her call you when I…when she wakes up." Alyssa took another drink, and the bowl was empty.

"Thank you, Alyssa. That would be wonderful. Oh, and get some sleep. You sound awful. If I didn't know you better, I'd think you were drinking."

She burst out laughing—a little too loud. "You know me. I won't touch the stuff." It was true; she hadn't touched it. She'd only drank it.

"Okay. Tell her I'm keeping my phone on me, and I'll answer her call no matter what time it is or what meeting I'm in."

"Will do."

"Bye, Alyssa."

"Talk to you later, Valerie." She put the phone away just as the waitress arrived with her nachos. She pushed the bowl aside. "Can I get a refill?"

Her eyes widened. "You already finished that? If you want more, I'll get you more."

"Can you make the next one a little stronger?"

"I...yeah. Okay." She gave Alyssa a concerned look and walked off.

Great. She was back to being a fragile doll. She picked up a chip covered in cheese. It was harder to get into her mouth than it should have been. Maybe she shouldn't have gone through the drink so fast. Who cared? At least she felt good, even if she still remembered why she had come here, and what she had been trying to forget.

She would keep drinking until she was able to forget for a little while. For now, she still knew her daughter was missing, even though it didn't feel as bad as it had earlier. She ate more nachos, focusing completely on that task since it was a bit of a challenge to get them into her mouth. She kept ending up with salsa on her face.

This was what she had come to.

Ride

ALYSSA LOOKED UP. A new fish bowl sat in front of her. When had that arrived? She grabbed the straw, drinking as much as she could. This batch was noticeably stronger. She drank until it was more than half-gone.

Alyssa blinked slowly, looking around. Her eyes wouldn't move fast at all. It was as though they had been put on a slow motion setting. Her arms didn't move as fast as she wanted, either. She looked at them as she moved around. They felt rubbery. It was a little bit fascinating.

She grabbed a chip, watching it in slow motion. It wouldn't go into her mouth, though. Somehow, she ended up with a sharp end of a chip up her nose, and it really hurt. Like, a lot. She put the chip down on the plate. It had red on it, but she didn't think that one had had any salsa on it. She rubbed her nose, and it felt squishy inside.

Something felt wet under her nose. It took a minute for her hand to get there, but she wiped it and saw red on her finger. That didn't look like salsa. She licked it. Ew. It definitely wasn't salsa. She had managed to give herself a bloody nose with a chip.

Someone sat next to her. She looked at him. He was tall and slim with curly hair and gorgeous eyes. He looked like he could have been on the cover of a magazine. "Who are you? What are you doing here?"

"Name's Rusty. I just want to make sure you're okay."

"Never better. I came here to forget something, and I can't remember what, so mission accomplished." She didn't like how slurred her words were. She reached for her straw, but the stranger moved the bowl away from her. "Hey." She glared at him.

"Maybe you should take a break from that for a minute."

"What's it to you?"

"You've had a lot already. You're a tiny thing. You can't be more than, what, a hundred and twenty pounds?"

"One twenty-five. What's it to you?"

"Just trying to look out for you."

"Why?"

"I'm a good citizen. Do you want me to get a napkin for your nose?"

She moved her rubber hand up to her nose, even though it took a long time. It was still wet. She shrugged, sure that she couldn't reach a napkin without knocking something over.

He handed her a couple napkins. How did he move so easily? It wasn't fair. Her body was made out of rubber and he moved like an Olympic athlete, in total control.

"What's your story?"

She raised an eyebrow, holding the napkin up to her nose.

"Why did you lie to your friend on the phone?"

"Did I lie? Was it that obvious?" She reached for the drink, but he pushed it further away. "Don't let that fall on the floor. I haven't even paid for that yet."

"I won't. You told your friend you were watching a movie."

Alyssa pointed to one of the TV's on the wall. "See? A movie. No lie."

"That's a replay of the NBA championship."

"Well, it's good enough to be a movie. Who did you say you were?"

"I'm Rusty. I've been trying to figure out what's going on with you."

"And I told you. I came here to forget something."

"You look familiar. Have we met?"

"I have one of those faces." There she was, lying again.

He nodded.

"Would you like a ride home?"

"I have my own car. I drove here."

"Do you think it would be such a good idea to drive it home? You can't even eat nachos without injuring yourself." He smiled. It was a beautiful smile. He probably had women lined up somewhere. What was he doing talking with her?

Alyssa glared at him. "I would hardly call it injuring myself. It's just a bloody nose."

"I wouldn't mind giving you a ride home. I couldn't live with myself if I let you get into your car in your state."

"Do I look like I'm ready to get back into my car? Hey—what's that?"

"What?" He turned around.

She grabbed the fish bowl and took another long sip.

He turned back and looked at her, shaking his head. Some curly locks fell into his eyes and he pushed them away. "Looks like you got me. Can I have some of that?"

"I don't know you. You could have all kinds of crazy germs."

He laughed. "Can I take that from you then? I'm afraid you're going to puke all that out."

"What's it to you? I'm not getting in your car."

"I think you should. I have a tow truck and I make a habit of offering free tows to those who shouldn't get on the road."

"Why? What's in it for you?"

"Plenty. I get to write off those tows on my taxes. More importantly, I save lives. Not only those poor souls who have had too much to drink, but also those they would have hurt or killed. That's why I hang out here in the wee hours."

"So you work all night doing that?"

"I work when I'm needed."

"Doesn't your family hate that?"

He shook his head, keeping her eye contact. "They were killed by a drunk driver years ago."

Alyssa dropped a chip she didn't even realize she was holding.

"I don't want anyone else to go through what I went through. I can't prevent them all, but I will prevent the ones I can."

She stared at him, at a loss for words. Finally, she pulled her cap off and ran her hands through her hair.

His eyes widened. "Wait. Are you that Mercer lady? Macy's mom?"

Alyssa put her hands in her face, fresh tears spilling. Even with all the alcohol she had consumed, she couldn't completely forget who she was or why she had gone to the bar. "Yes. I'm Alyssa Mercer. My daughter is missing, and we're all over the news. Looks like you figured out why I came here." She grabbed the drink and downed the rest of it before he could try to take it away. "And I can't forget it."

"You know, drinking isn't going to solve anything."

She stared at him through the tears. "Who asked you?"

"No one. I'm offering you unsolicited advice. Get counseling, but don't turn to alcohol. Please."

Alyssa sighed. "I don't even have closure. We don't know if she's dead or alive. They found her bloody clothes. Did you know that? The results just came back today. Someone broke into our house last night, too…or was it the night before?" She shook her head. "It doesn't matter. My life is falling apart, and if I want some alcohol, I'll have as much as I want. I'm sorry for everything you've been through. I'm sure it was as bad of a nightmare as my life, but you still don't get the privilege of telling me what to do."

He pulled a wallet out from his pocket and showed her a picture of his family. Alyssa held her breath as she stared at the photo of him with an equally gorgeous lady and two beautiful boys, no older than five.

Her breath caught. "They're gone?"

Rusty nodded, a look of sadness shadowing his face. "Have you ever been to a rehab facility?"

"What? No."

"Trust me, Alyssa. You don't want to. I turned to drugs, unable to cope with losing my family. I ended up almost losing my house, my job, and everything else. I didn't care. I couldn't get over the grief, and nothing else mattered."

"I don't want to hear this. This is the first drink I've touched in a long time. I think I deserve a drink after the week I've had."

"And I don't want to see you go down the path I did."

"Why do you care? You don't know me."

"I kind of do. I've been sitting here with you for a little bit."

The waitress came by and looked at Alyssa. "Do you need anything else?"

"Just another one of those fishb—"

"She needs some water."

"No, I don't. I want another bowl." She'd show him.

He shook his head. "I'm going to take her home. She's already had too much."

The waitress shrugged. "Water it is, Rusty."

Alyssa groaned. She couldn't even go to a bar and get drunk right. Her stomach didn't feel well. It wasn't exactly growling, but she couldn't ignore it, so she grabbed a few chips and managed to eat them without hurting herself. The waitress brought two waters and left without a word. At least the tow truck guy had stopped talking.

What if he went out and told everyone that he had found her drunk? Her stomach dropped. The media would eat them alive. "You're not going to tell the news that you found me drunk in a bar, are you? That's going to make my family look really bad. I don't—"

"No. I just want to help. I know what it's like to deal with grief that's too overwhelming."

She looked into his eyes, not able to focus on them. He seemed genuine enough. Hopefully he was. If he drove her anywhere other than her house, she wouldn't be able to fight him off. Not when her extremities were rubbery.

Her stomach continued to feel strange. She stuffed more nachos in her mouth, trying to appease it. Just before she finished off the plate, her stomach twisted in knots and heaved. She was going to throw up.

Alyssa covered her mouth and looked around, afraid she wouldn't find the bathroom in time.

"Over there to the right. Let me help you—"

She jumped out of her seat and ran to the restroom, barely making it in time. She threw up so much, she was sure it was everything she'd put in her stomach since arriving at the bar. That wasn't money well-spent.

By the time she got to the table, only the waters remained.

"Do you feel better now?"

She shook her head as she sat down.

"Whenever you're ready to go, just say the word."

"I guess I should get back home. I threw everything up. I can get myself home."

"No, you can't. All that alcohol is still in your blood."

She knew he was right, because she still felt dizzy and rubbery.

"Are you ready? The sooner I get you home, the sooner I can get home."

"May as well. I need to get back before anyone wakes up. I don't want to explain myself." She opened her purse to pay for her purchase.

"I already paid your bill."

She looked up at him. "You did? Why?"

"Consider it my good deed for the day."

A headache was coming on. "I could have paid it."

"I'm sure you could have. Find something good to put the money toward. Buy something for your son."

Alex. Hopefully, he would be sleeping when she got back. The last thing he needed was to see his mom coming home drunk, especially with some guy named Rusty dropping her off. "Let's go."

She took in the fresh night air as she watched him attach her car to the back of his truck. When he was done, he turned to her. "All set. You ready to go?"

"So, do I get in my car?"

He gave her a funny look. "Haven't you been towed before? You ride in my cab with me."

"Cab?" She looked around for a taxi.

Rusty pointed to the front of his truck. "Just climb in."

She nodded, feeling stupid. He opened the door, and she put her foot on the step. Her foot slipped, and she slammed her shin against the step. That would leave a mark. Possibly even blood.

He took her arm and helped her up. A couple of minutes later, they were driving back toward her house. She looked back several times to check on her car.

"It's fine. I know what I'm doing—really. I even have a license and everything."

"Sorry."

"No need to apologize. Do you want to give me your address to put in my GPS or do you just want to give me directions?"

If she gave him her address, he would have it permanently. Did she really want that? Or did it even matter? He would be able to figure it out once he got there. The headache was getting worse, and she didn't want to have to think. She told him the address, and closed her eyes. Hopefully, that would help. If not, at least it would keep the lights outside from making her feel dizzy as they drove past.

What had she been thinking? Why had she drunk so much?

Soon, the brakes hissed. She opened her eyes and saw her house. Had she fallen asleep? Is that how they had gotten back so fast?

He pulled the keys out of the ignition. “Let me help you get out. It’s a big drop, and I don’t want you getting hurt.”

“You think I’m an idiot, don’t you?” Oh, why had she said that?

“Not at all. I just don’t want you injuring yourself. Just wait in here while I take care of your car.”

She sighed and then waited. With any luck, no neighbors were awake to watch. There were several who loved to gossip, and they would eat this up—her arriving early in the morning in a tow truck. She looked at the windows she could see, but everything looked as it should: no nosy neighbors peeking from behind any curtains.

Her door opened, and Rusty put his hand out for her to take. With his help, she managed to get out onto the street without any more blood.

“Do you want me to leave your car here, by the sidewalk? I can put it up your driveway if you’d like.”

Chad would know something wasn’t right if her car was parked on the road. He wouldn’t think anything of it being in the driveway, because half the time she didn’t bother putting it in the garage anyway. She sighed and then handed him her keys.

When he was done parking the car, he returned the keys to her. He gave her a nod, his eyes full of kindness. “I hope you find your daughter soon. In the meantime, please don’t turn to drinking.”

She rubbed her head. “Not if it keeps feeling like this.”

“Glad to hear it. Have a good night.”

“Wait. Let me pay you something.”

“No. Like I told you, it’s a write-off. You’re helping me out with tax time coming up.”

“But you covered my food too.”

“It’s all a write-off. Just get in there and get some sleep. You’re going to need it.”

"Okay. Thanks."

"Goodnight."

Alyssa walked to her front door. When she got there, she turned around and saw that Rusty was sitting in his truck, watching her. Was he making sure she could get into her house? She must have been in pretty bad shape if he doubted her ability to do that. She pulled out her key and unlocked the door.

She turned around and waved, letting him know he was free to go. Then she opened the door and went in, resetting the alarm. She was half-surprised that she remembered the new codes, but at least she did.

The house was quiet and it was still dark. No one had any reason to get up early, so she was probably safe from having to explain herself.

When she got into her room, she let a sigh of relief seeing Chad in the same position he had been in when she left. She got in the shower to wash off the smells from the night.

She climbed into bed, her hair still wet, and she relaxed. Her stomach was still queasy, but the alcohol had done the job of calming her nerves. Things didn't look as bad as they had before. She could see that there was no evidence of foul play, so she had reason to cling to hope that she would see Macy again.

Alyssa closed her eyes and for the first time in a while, drifted off to sleep without any anxious thoughts haunting her.

Clue

THE SUN WAS shining into the room through the blinds. One ray of light made its way to Chad's eyes, waking him up. He rubbed his eyes and looked around. It was pretty bright, which meant that it had to be late morning. He looked over at Alyssa, sleeping soundly next to him.

How odd that she was still sleeping. She had never been one to sleep in to begin with, always off to work out or something. Now that Macy was missing, she usually got up even earlier. He knew she hadn't been sleeping well. She tended to talk in her sleep—she had as long as he had known her—but it had been much worse over the last week.

She had woken him up several times yelling out, though she hadn't managed to wake herself.

He got up, put on some track pants and an old college sweatshirt, and went into the hall. Both Alex's door and the door to Macy's room, where Zoey slept, were still closed. Not that that was a surprise. He remembered sleeping well past noon often as a teenager.

His stomach rumbled, so he went to the kitchen. He looked at the clock on the stove. It was almost eleven, which meant he may as well make lunch. He remembered the leftover lasagna. He would never be able to eat lasagna without guilt again. There was no way he was ever going to tell Alyssa about Lydia, but since he was never going to go back to her again, it didn't matter. The past was in the past.

Chad grabbed the tinfoil-covered dish from the fridge and piled a huge piece onto a plate. He stuck it in the microwave and waited. He looked through the fridge for something to drink. He was too awake for coffee, which was his usual morning fuel. Milk? No, it gave him gas. He didn't want to spend the whole day farting. Juice? Too sweet. Beer? Bingo.

He grabbed a bottle and opened it up just as the microwave beeped. He sat down with his lasagna and beer. The breakfast of champions. It was perfect, actually. Once he got to the middle of his food, it was cold, so he had to put it back in for another couple of minutes. He finished the beer while he waited.

Once the food was done, it was too hot. Stupid microwaves. He put the plate on a potholder and carried it to his office. He'd let it cool down while he checked the comments on his blog.

His latest post had over two hundred new comments. Not surprising since he hadn't checked in a while. Had he even checked the day before?

He read through the comments, answering each one. They were all typical as of late. Mostly condolences for what their family was going through. Those were easy enough to reply to. A simple thank you sufficed in most cases. Occasionally, someone had something special to say, and he needed to give it extra attention.

He went through the rest of the comments on the post and then checked for other new comments on other posts. There were about eighty other comments to answer. After he was done with that, he needed to write a new post. People would stop checking if he didn't update soon.

Once he had replied to the last comment, he checked all the local news blogs. They all mentioned the bloody clothes. Each one of them made it sound like there was a lot more blood than there actually was. He checked a couple of the national news sites, and they both said the same thing.

Oddly enough, none of his blog comments had mentioned it, so the news must have just been released.

He opened up a new post and let his fingers do the talking. He let the public know everything that he did. Yes, they found Macy's clothes covered in blood, but it wasn't nearly enough to be deadly. He suspected a cut, and would believe that until other evidence proved otherwise.

Before hitting publish, he went through pictures on his computer. Family pictures brought in a lot more visitors, and he wanted everyone to know the truth. He uploaded a dozen pictures, all including Macy, from the last ten years or so. People couldn't get enough of that.

Chad hit publish and then checked the live post. Even though he always previewed it first, he sometimes managed to catch errors that he'd missed. This one looked good.

Not only did he have high numbers, but he had a program showing how many times his content was shared, and his posts were getting shared thousands of times each week. That wasn't even counting all the re-blogs, which he didn't have time to track.

He refreshed the page and saw there were already comments. People had to have been sitting on his site, waiting for the latest bit of news. It was a good thing he had already upgraded his hosting to handle all the traffic.

Leaning back in his chair, he stretched. He would read the comments later. He needed to get his mind off everything. The worry and guilt ate away at his stomach. As much as he wanted to spend every waking minute focused on finding Macy, he needed breaks from it all.

It made him feel like a first-class jerk, but he knew that he was no good to anyone if he didn't take breaks. He went upstairs and found that he was still the only one awake. He ran a brush and some gel through his hair and headed outside for a walk.

He walked mindlessly through the neighborhood, purposefully avoiding the park. The last thing he wanted was to run into anyone, and as much as he appreciated everyone's efforts with the search parties, he couldn't do it right then. Maybe he could find a clue wandering through the neighborhood.

Eventually Chad's calves felt sore. He was going up an incline, and looked around to see where he was. He'd been so lost in his thoughts, he hadn't been paying any attention. The way the roads were set up, he was actually heading back home. It would take him longer to get there if he turned around.

"Is that you, Chad?"

Turning around, he prepared himself. He knew that voice anywhere. "Lydia."

She had dirt on her knees and held clippers. "What are you doing over here?"

"Just trying to clear my head."

"I like to get outside for that myself. Even though we have a landscaper, I like to come out and work on the rose bushes."

"They look great. I should get home, though. I'm sure my family will be waking up soon."

"You look thirsty. Want to come in for a drink?"

"I really shouldn't."

"Well, let me bring something out for you. You need to take care of yourself."

"Lydia, I—"

"Just let me grab something. I know what you like."

"Okay." He sighed.

She came back with two of his favorite diet sodas and handed him one.

"Thanks." Chad didn't realize how thirsty he was until he started drinking. He had finished the entire thing in a couple gulps.

Lydia smiled at him. "See? I knew you were thirsty."

He nodded. "I appreciate it. Really, though, I should get going."

She took his empty bottle and held his eye contact. "If you need anything, anything at all, don't be afraid to ask. I'll do anything for you."

"You've done plenty. We all enjoyed the lasagna, even though we were upset about the news."

She nodded, and then stepped closer. "Are your needs being met? I've always been able to—"

"I told you, I'm working things out with Alyssa."

"Of course. But after speaking with her, it's obvious that she's consumed with grief. It would help you to talk with someone neutral. Our heart-to-heart discussions are second to none." She stepped even closer.

Chad swallowed, still looking her in the eyes. He couldn't deny what she said, but that was the problem. If he opened himself to her he would put his relationship with Alyssa on the line. He would destroy his family.

"Chad?" Lydia put her hand on his.

Some of her hair fell into her face. Without thinking, Chad reached out to brush it behind her ear.

"What do you say?" Her voice was soft, and he could feel her breath on his face. She smelled sweet, even though she had been out doing yard work. "Come inside and tell me everything."

His breath caught, and for a moment he considered taking her up on the offer. Alyssa and the kids didn't deserve this. He needed to give Alex a good home life now more than ever. And Macy…he didn't want her coming back to a broken family, which is what would eventually happen if he didn't stay away from Lydia. He couldn't have both, and he knew it.

"Well?"

Chad stepped back. "Lydia, you're a sweet person. It kills me that Dean can't see that, but I need to be there for my family—all of them. Thanks again for the drink."

Disappointment washed over her face.

"I'm sorry. I never wanted to hurt you."

She nodded, and then waved. "You know where to find me."

Surprise

ALYSSA WOKE UP, unsure if the pounding came from her head or outside somewhere. The light was blinding and it hurt—a lot. She needed some powerful painkillers. With any luck, her stomach would be able to handle them. After throwing up the previous night, she was certain there was nothing left in her stomach to worry about vomiting.

Maybe she should eat something first. Aspirin on an empty stomach would cause more problems than she already had. She grabbed a bottle from the bathroom and headed down to the kitchen. She grabbed some frozen pancakes and put them in the microwave.

The house was quiet. Chad was probably working on his blog and the kids were probably still sleeping. Not that she could blame them, especially after getting up so late herself.

She had acted like an idiot the night before, running off and getting drunk. She hadn't done that since college, and even then it had been with friends. At this age, she was just pathetic. She needed to pull herself together. She'd already lost Macy—hopefully only for a time—and she needed to be there for Alex. He needed her more than ever, even though he acted tough.

The microwave beeped, indicating the food was ready. She took the steaming plate out and set it on the counter while she started a pot of coffee. That would help her headache. She usually tried not to drink too much of it, but she also didn't usually drink fish bowls full of alcohol, either. How many had she had?

Guilt hit her as she remembered the night before. What had she been thinking? What if Chad noticed her car was out of the garage? What would she tell him? The last thing she wanted to do was admit to the truth. He would understand drinking; he always kept beer in the fridge. But he didn't get drunk.

He was practically the perfect husband, and she hadn't let herself see that in a long time. He not only worked a high-paying job so their family never lacked anything, but he put nearly as many hours into the blog. Never once did he ask her to even get a part-time job so he could focus on it. Instead, he spent countless hours working while she complained about him not caring.

What had she been thinking?

The front door opened. Had he gone somewhere? She pushed the brew button on the coffee pot and went to see. Their eyes met, and he held her gaze.

"I needed some air, so I went for a walk."

Alyssa nodded. "I made some coffee. Do you want some?"

He wrapped his arms around her. "I love you. I'm sorry that I wasn't there for you when you needed me."

She hugged him back. "What do you mean?"

"Before. You know, when things were normal. I was so busy, I never made any time for you or the kids."

She leaned her head against his shoulder. "No. I'm sorry that I didn't appreciate all the work you were doing for our family. I haven't had to work in years, and yet you've worked so hard and asked for nothing in return."

"I wouldn't say 'nothing.' And you've given much more than I ever stopped to notice as well. You take such good care of the kids, always going to their school events. I should have been there with you."

"You were…sometimes."

"That's not good enough."

"I obviously didn't do that great of a job with the kids. Look what happened to Macy."

Chad stepped back, looking her directly in the eyes. He cupped her face and held on. "That isn't your fault. We don't know what happened. Sure, we could have been less strict, but you know what? We were trying to protect them. We were doing our job. She's out there somewhere, and we'll find her. Together."

Alyssa nodded. "Together."

Tired

MACY SAT UP in bed, gasping for air. She looked around the room, relieved to be there. She had dreamed of being back in the barn.

The teddy bear was still gone. She wanted to hold it and smell her house, her real house. Would she ever see it again? Would she see her family again? She missed them so much it hurt.

What she wouldn't have given to have Alex tease her, trying to rile her up. Who would have ever thought she would miss that? She would love nothing more than to walk into her dad's office and ask him about his blog. His face always lit up when he talked about page views and other stuff that Macy really didn't understand. She loved to see him excited. If she could, she would walk into her parents' room and for once, agree to go to the gym with her mom.

Macy had always been worried that someone from school might see her and make fun of her. She would never live down her nickname, and she had been afraid that going to the gym would be like admitting all those jerks had been right.

Now she might never have the chance to do that again. Any of it. Was her dad still working on his blog? Were they so worried about her that they weren't doing anything they loved? What did they think about the bloody clothes? Did they think she was dead? Would they really give up on her and move on? What if they moved away? How would she ever find them?

Tears filled her eyes. She wiped them away. Even if she had to wait a few years to get away, she would find her parents as soon as she could.

He couldn't have been more than fifty, if he was even that old. He looked older than her dad, but that didn't mean much. What if he was only forty-five? He could have a lot of years left in him. She didn't want to have to spend the next forty or fifty years with him.

What exactly was he planning? Whatever it was, she had to go along with it or she would end up in worse shape than before. He made things worse on her each time. She didn't want to find out what could be worse than being tied up for days.

If he wanted to her to become Heather, he had won. Just like a wild horse, she was broken. Whatever he said, she would do.

Macy decided to look for the bear again, even though she doubted she would find it. It was probably in his room, along with the picture of her family. He had made his point more than clear. She wasn't going anywhere near his room ever again. She rubbed her wrists, which were still sore from the ties. Chester made her wear shirts with sleeves so long they nearly reached her knuckles so his parents wouldn't see the marks.

Looking around the room, she tried to figure out where to look first. There was a pile of stuffed animals in a little toy hammock. That would be the obvious place to look, so it would be the last place. She continued to scan the room, and she stopped at the dresser. She had already gone through it, hoping to find better clothing options.

For some reason she couldn't explain, she wanted to look there again. The teddy probably wouldn't fit in any of the drawers with all the clothes in there, but she couldn't shake the feeling, so she walked over to it. Starting with the top drawer, she went through each one, not finding the bear.

Frowning, she closed the bottom drawer. Why had she been so sure she would find it? The drawer stuck halfway. She pushed harder, but it wouldn't budge. She stuck her hands in it, pushing all the clothes down. One of them was probably stuck and causing the problem.

She pushed again, but it still wouldn't move. Something was blocking it, but it wasn't coming from inside the drawer. Could it be something under the drawer?

Macy pulled the drawer out further and positioned herself so she could reach behind it. Something was back there. She felt it with her hand as best as she could. It almost felt like part of the dresser. She managed to wrap her fingers around it. Was it another diary? Had Heather hidden one there, too?

Scratching her hand along the way, she managed to pull it out of the drawer. It did look like a diary! Would this one tell her more than the last one had? Heather's mom had spent some time in the cellar, but what had *happened* to them? Where were they now?

Macy leaned against the wall next to the dresser, so she would be hidden if Chester came in. She opened the book to the first entry.

Mom still hasn't come back. I still don't know exactly what she meant when she said she had been at Grandma and Grandpa's barn. She didn't say farm, she said barn. Why would she be in their barn all that time? They love her. Grandma always says Mom's the daughter she never had. Why would they make her stay out in the barn? Couldn't they see what it did to her?

I'll never know, because Dad won't let me call them. He took my cell phone away when he walked in on me calling them—he took it right out of my hand, ended the call, and removed the battery. Then he told me I'd never see it again. He said that would teach me to ask questions I had no business asking.

No business? He's insane. Of course I have business asking questions. He should be asking questions too! Mom's missing and he doesn't even care. How can he not be worried? I'm so scared I've been throwing up. Not that he cares. I know he can hear me, but he acts like nothing's wrong.

I even threw up a bunch of times at school and Sierra told Mr. Lee who took me to the school nurse. She called Dad and he told her I was fine. It was just a stomach bug. She told him I needed to go home, but Dad said he wouldn't authorize it. So the nurse had me stay in her office the rest of the day to keep an eye on me.

She was asking all kinds of questions about my home life and I was being as vague as possible. After Dad's threats to stay quiet, I wasn't going to say anything.

Macy put the diary in her lap. What had Chester threatened her with? Was there another diary that Macy hadn't read? The other one she had read didn't say anything about it other than the fact that he didn't want her talking about their family at school. She had also said that she was scared of the look on his face. That hadn't been a threat, though.

There was guilt stabbing at me right in my chest and stomach. What if Mom was in danger? Would it be better for me to say something so she could get help, even though Dad said he would lock me away and move me away from my friends? Would he really do that? I'm such a coward.

I couldn't get the look in Dad's eyes out of my mind. I wish I could explain it—the way just him looking at me made terror run through me. I never knew what the expression "frozen with fear" meant until he gave me that look. That's exactly how I felt, and even feel now thinking about it.

Before Mom disappeared again, she told me that if she disappeared again, I needed to take care of myself. She was speaking pretty cryptically, but it seemed like she didn't want me telling anyone about her being missing. I think she was worried about me.

If I'm frozen with fear, then Mom was paralyzed with it. Like I said in the other diaries, she never went back into her and Dad's room. Even though she talked with me, I don't think she ever talked to him. She definitely wouldn't look at him.

One day, she whispered something about a gun. What did that mean? I couldn't get her to tell me anything else, and I didn't know what she was talking about. Did Dad get one and that was why she was so scared?

Ugh. I'm rambling. Sierra and Jess keep saying I do that too much lately. Talking about one thing and then another, but not really getting anywhere. Either it's from spending all that time with Mom when she was back or I'm losing it too.

What am I supposed to do?! I mean, seriously. What? Mom's gone again—just when she was starting to return to her normal self. Dad has to be behind it. Otherwise he would at least pretend to give a crap. He won't even do that. What kind of a husband doesn't care that his wife is missing?

He's back to saying she's in Paris. That's a load bull crap and he knows it. I nearly said as much, but I thought he was going to hit me, so I stopped. I hate him. I really do. Mom always says I shouldn't hate anyone, that it'll make me sick and won't hurt the other person. What am I supposed to do, though?

I need to say something to someone. I have to. Whatever's going on with Mom is not right. People don't just disappear like she does. At least she *doesn't do that. Maybe others do, but not her. Something is wrong, wrong, wrong. What if she comes back in worse shape than before? Like, what if she stops talking altogether? Or worse, what if she doesn't come back at all?*

There's no way I could handle that. I just couldn't. There's no way I would survive. I'm barely holding it together now. I have tightness in my chest most of the time and my stomach hurts something awful. Jess says it's ulcers. She would know, her mom's a wreck. She says stress eats holes in your stomach. Maybe that's it. It doesn't matter, not when something is really wrong with my mom.

She needs me. I have to say something. Who do I talk to? Mr. Lee? The school nurse? The school psychiatrist? Dad already told me I better not ever talk to her. He says that our family doesn't need that kind of a reputation. Also, he said that his daughter doesn't need a shrink. Ha! Who else needs professional help than anyone with direct contact with him? I'll probably spend all of my adult life in counseling, trying to heal from everything I've been through lately.

There I go rambling again. I'm shaking too. I need to tell someone. I know it and I have to be willing to face the consequences. I can't sit around doing nothing while Mom needs something. I don't know where she is, but maybe someone could look in Gram's barn.

I wish I had my phone. I would call the cops. There's not even a landline here. Dad got rid of that when I was little. I never really thought about it, but now that I needed to make a call and don't have my phone, I'm stuck. Can I really wait until tomorrow at school? What if that's too late for Mom? I know she needs me.

Macy read four more pages of Heather's ramblings. Not that she minded, or even blamed her. If Macy had a diary of her own, it would probably be a lot worse than what she was reading. Heather actually seemed to be holding it together pretty well, considering everything.

When she got to the next entry, the handwriting was a lot messier. Something had to be seriously wrong.

Macy flipped the diary page, eager to find out why Heather's handwriting looked so distressed.

I really messed things up. Really bad this time. Dad's going to follow through on his threat for sure now. He's going to lock me away. He told me that I'm never going to see my friends again.

Today at school, I decided to talk to Mr. Lee. He could tell that something was wrong, so he called me to his desk during the quiz. He asked how I was, but I think it was pretty clear. I was shaking and I hadn't put on any makeup, so it was obvious, really obvious.

He took me into the hall and by then I was shaking so bad I could barely stand. He told me to sit down and then he sat next to me, asking questions. It reminded me of when I was on the couch with Mom when she wouldn't talk. Only I was on the other side. I couldn't find my voice, and even if I had been able to, I'm not sure I would've known what to say.

How would I explain everything that was going on? Where would I even start? Mr. Lee kept asking questions, and I just shook harder and harder. I needed to say something for Mom's sake. She needed me to. So, I finally found my voice and told him that Mom was missing again.

I can't remember what happened after that. Like, I literally can't remember a single thing. All I know is that somehow I ended up in the psychiatrist's office. She was asking questions about Mom. I was crying too hard to answer any questions.

At some point, the new principal came in. He said something about CPS. I asked if they were going to help find Mom. He said that they would help me. I stood up and screamed that I didn't need help. I threw my fists up and down, shouting that they needed to help Mom. I was fine—at least compared to her!

Both of them held me down in the chair, but I kept screaming all the more, so loud that my throat still hurts. Why wouldn't they listen to me? I wasn't the one who needs help. Well, I do. Not as much as Mom. They need to focus on getting her home safe.

I needed to make them listen to me. I kept kicking and trying to get my arms loose. They were holding me down so tightly that I still have marks. Anyway, I finally calmed down once I figured out that they wouldn't listen to me until I did. Yelling and thrashing around wasn't getting me anywhere so I had to try talking calmly.

So long story short, now I'm home in my room and Dad's talking to the CPS people. I'm supposed to be packing some clothes and anything soft I might need. I'm going somewhere for observation, apparently. I hope they have a search team looking for Mom. They need to forget about me and find her. Can't they see that? I'm here and she's not.

The look in Dad's eyes is even scarier than before. He's beyond furious. There's not even a word to describe how angry he is.

I just snuck out into the hall and listened to what they were saying. They're going to take me to the mental hospital! Holy crap! The loony bin. They think I'm nuts. No! He's the one who needs to go there. Why can't they see that? But on the bright side, at least I'll be safe from Dad. They'll figure out that I'm not the crazy one. I'll just have to stay calm and not scream and shout like I did at school. The truth will come out.

Well, I just listened again because I heard Dad yelling. One of the CPS guys said something to Dad about watching out or he'd lose custody. Does that mean that they would take me away from him?

Then Mom and I could move away and then…

Discussion

MACY FLIPPED THE page, but the rest of the diary was blank. Why had Heather stopped in the middle of a sentence? Had she heard them coming for her and hidden the diary behind the drawer where Macy had found it?

Where *was* she? Was Heather in the mental facility? Did they take her there and leave her? Or had they taken away Chester's custody and put her up for adoption or foster care?

Had he tried to get her back, but couldn't? Was that why he went after Macy? Because he couldn't get to Heather?

She sighed, flipping through the entries again, looking for anything she might have missed before. There weren't any clues that she could find, tucked away out of plain sight.

Even though there were a lot of unanswered questions, Macy understood more about the entire situation. Something happened between Heather's parents to make Chester snap and put her mother in the barn, not just once but at least twice. There seemed to be a missing diary, so he may have taken her there more than once.

Had he tied her up like he had with Macy? He must have threatened her because why else would she have sat there, not talking to Heather? Either she really was that traumatized, or she had been trying to protect Heather. Being down there was horrible, but bad enough to stare at the wall for days on end?

Unless living with Chester all those years had done it to her. It could have been the final straw for her, and she snapped. Heather had snapped too, screaming at school. Had anyone at the mental hospital believed her about her mom? They must not have if Chester was wandering around free. Did he convince them about the Paris story, too?

Although they weren't staying at the family house—the one Heather had been dragged away from. Had Chester packed everything in a hurry, moving it back to his parents' house after losing custody? He had to have lost custody; otherwise he wouldn't have gone to the effort of taking Macy.

What if somehow Macy could find Heather? It was obviously a long shot, but if Heather had gotten away maybe Macy could too. Except that Chester would be even more careful in the future. He had already gone to great lengths to make sure Macy would do what he said.

She heard something in the hall, so she slid the diary back behind the dresser. It barely fit. She jumped up and pretended to be looking through the drawer that was still pulled out.

The door opened, but she pretended not to notice. Her heart raced again. She held up a pair of pants, pretending to decide whether or not to wear them.

Chester cleared his throat. Heart pounding, Macy turned and looked at him, forcing her face to look neutral.

He smiled. "Good morning, sunshine."

Macy's eyes widened. She couldn't find her voice.

"Mind if I sit?" His expression was relaxed.

She stared, afraid to speak. After everything she'd just read she had nothing to say. Where would she even begin?

He sat on the bed and then patted the quilt. Did he want her to sit next to him?

"Have a seat, Heather."

Macy put the pants back into the drawer and walked over to the bed. She looked at it, not wanting to sit.

Chester patted the bed again.

Afraid to anger him, Macy sat without a word.

"I know things have been rough, but we'll get through it. Everything is going to turn around, don't you agree?"

She looked at him, her eyes widening even further. The only way they would get better was if he would take her back home. She knew that wasn't what he had planned. Not if he was still calling her Heather.

"We can be a happy family now. You know your place, as everyone should. You're being more respectful, not like your mom was before she ran off to Paris. Maybe she'll even come to her senses and come back. Then we could be a complete family again. What do you think?"

Macy's breath caught, still unable to find her voice.

He gave her a sad smile and put his hand on her knee. "Yeah, I don't hold out much hope, either. That doesn't mean that we can't be happy. You and me, we're still together. Your grandparents are happy to have us here, and though we don't want to overstay our welcome, we can build a new sense of normal. Does that sound good?"

She bit her lip. How was she supposed to react to that? Did he really believe what he was saying, or was he only trying to get her to believe it?

Chester removed his hand from her knee. "I know. It's not perfect. As much as you've always loved being here, it isn't home. We just need this time away from everything to rebuild our family. After everything we've been through, we have to band together and get through it together. Things aren't going to be the same with your mom gone, and we can't pretend otherwise. She's gone, and there's nothing we can do about that."

He sighed and looked around the room, giving Macy a little space to breathe. Where was he going with all of this talk? Did it mean he was done locking her up? All she would have to do was pretend to be obedient, and she might get a little freedom? Would he be nice now that he deemed her changed?

Turning to her, he smiled again. It caught her off-guard. It would have been less worrisome if he was being mean. "What are you thinking, Heather?"

She held his eye contact, still not knowing what to say. What if she said the wrong thing and ended up back in the barn again? Would he leave her longer? She couldn't have taken any more. Would he leave her there permanently, trying to find yet another Heather, this time one who would be more agreeable?

"It's a lot to take in, I know. Especially with your mom gone now. You two were close, but you know what? This gives us room to be closer. We've never been as close as I would have liked. It's a chance for us to turn over a new leaf. Isn't that exciting?"

Macy could see the eagerness in his eyes. She knew she had no choice except to respond. She nodded.

"Can't you say anything? I'm excited, and you can't even find one word?"

Certain she could hear irritation creeping into his tone, she knew she had to say something, even if it was a bold-faced lie. She couldn't go back into the cellar. "It'll be great. It's something we've never done before." At least the second part was true. Even with as horrible as he had been to her, she still hated lying.

He broke into a huge grin, his entire face changing. For that moment, he didn't look like the scary monster who had tortured her. He looked like a broken man finding a ray of hope. Macy almost felt sorry for him—almost.

Chester pulled her into a hug, squishing her face against his side. "This is a new beginning for us, kid. Things are really going to turn around. Even though things have been rough, we're going to be able to become a happy little family again. Life is going to be good again. Right, honey?"

Macy's eyes widened. Did he really expect her to agree with that?

He squeezed her tighter into the hug. "Right?"

"Yeah, Dad. It's going to be great." Macy rolled her eyes.

"I'm so glad to have you back, Heather."

Goodbye

CHESTER WALKED ALONG the overgrown path, his boots catching on loose pricker vines along the way. The trees overhead cast a dark shadow, giving him the chills. He should have grabbed a coat rather than just the flannel.

He looked at his watch. Forty-five minutes since he had left the farmhouse. Only another seven minutes before he arrived. She would wait as long as he took.

The forest was quiet, but that wasn't unusual for this time of year. The birds had flown south for the nearing winter, and the critters were all building their homes. A fat squirrel ran in front of Chester, chattering away. By springtime, they would all be skinny again.

It wouldn't be long now. Probably only three more minutes—no point in checking the time again. He took a deep breath, starting to feel winded. At least this trip was easier than the first one out there. Carrying all that added weight had made the trip more than twice as long.

Three rocks piled on top of each other, leaning against a hollowed out stump, reminded him to turn left. The pricker bushes were thick to keep the path hidden. Not that many people went this deep into the woods to begin with.

Chester leaned against the nearest tree, mentally preparing himself for the last leg of this relatively small journey. He kicked some frost on the ground as he thought about what he was going to say to her. It was going to be pivotal, as this would be goodbye.

He pulled some thorns from his boots before knocking over the pile of three rocks. He wouldn't need those again, and he certainly didn't need anyone else seeing them and figuring out that they pointed somewhere.

The rocks sent dirt and frost flying in all directions.

He made his way to the hidden path, making sure there was no exposed skin between the thick, leather gloves and his flannel shirt.

A thick, curved stick sat at the base of one tree where he had left it last time. He picked it up and pushed aside the thorn bushes, allowing himself through. The branches snagged his back as they fell back into place behind him. His clothes would be snagged up, but that wasn't of any concern. He'd picked them just for this occasion.

Finally he made it to the small clearing. Frost covered the ground here more than anywhere else in the woods. Little footprints indicated small critters running through.

Four rocks piled on top of one another caught his attention. They sat off to the right of the field, looking sad and solitary. There she was, waiting for him. His heart picked up speed, and he walked over to her. He fell to his knees in front of the rocks. Tears shone in his eyes as he sat above her where she rested.

"Karla, my dear. How I've missed you. Have you missed me? I suppose you have, since you haven't had any other visitors." He pulled off his cap, raking his fingers through his hair, before replacing it. "It's been a while. I apologize for that, because I know you want answers. You wish Heather could be with you, but that isn't possible, my dear. I've gotten her back. Can you believe that?"

He paused, listening.

"She was mad at first, but who could blame her? I think she's missed you, but it's hard to say. She hasn't really asked about you. I wouldn't have told you—I know hearing that has to hurt—but it's the truth. She just hasn't asked. I had to put her in the barn a couple of times. I know how much you hate that. That was part of the problem, you know? You just had such a hard time accepting my decisions. I wish that hadn't been the case."

Chester removed his gloves and ran his hand along the frosty dirt, remembering how he used to enjoy running his hands along her back. "I don't know why you couldn't just accept my leadership. Why wouldn't you listen to me? Now you have no choice, and I wish you would have chosen your path when...before, my dear Karla. I would so much rather have you at my side, but you just wouldn't listen." He shook his head, feeling choked up.

"It's such a shame. Such a shame. Heather needs a mom, and she's looking for something. I can see it in her eyes. She knows I'm her dad. I love how it rolls off her tongue so naturally now. But my dear, we're not a family. Not without you. She knows it, even though she won't say anything. I wish she would ask about you, because then I wouldn't have to hurt you with the knowledge that she hasn't said anything. You two were so close, do you remember?"

He patted the ground as though patting her back. "Well, the truth is that life must move on. We don't have you with us, as much as I wish we did. Wishing doesn't make it so, just like that book you always used to read Heather when she was little. Do you remember that? Of course you do. It was about sinks, and you bought it before she was even born. I put the book aside, and I'll bring it back out and remind her when she's ready. For now, I think it's too painful for her to think about you."

His knees ached, so he readjusted. "I can't stay long, Karla. I'm not as young as I used to be. This is goodbye. Please don't cry—it has to be this way. Think of Heather. We need to move on, and we can't stay with my parents much longer. She's beginning to understand what you never would: the importance of following my leadership, and the fact that there are serious consequences for not doing so. Rebellion is not accepted. You know that now, don't you?"

Chester raised his hand to his face, kissed two fingers, and then placed them on the ground. "I can't say whether or not I'll ever be back. I hope so—I hate the thought of never seeing you again. You will always be my one true love. Please don't forget that. No matter what happens, I'll never be able to love another like I loved you. So rest sweetly, and don't get your hopes up. I wouldn't want you agonizing for me. Just expect that I won't return. It's for the best, as much as I know you wish I would stay."

He ran his fingers in a zig-zag pattern along the frosty dirt, thinking of all the times he had made the same pattern on her back. "We'll miss each other, but Heather needs us to move on. There are too many memories here. I haven't decided what to do with our house, either, Karla. What do you think? Should I keep renting it out, or should I sell it? The renters keep asking about buying it. Again, there are so many memories. I don't know if I dare bring Heather back there. What if she regresses? She's finally doing so well. She's really becoming obedient, you know? I'm raising her to be the way a woman should be. No stupid questions. Just sweet submission."

The sun had risen over the clearing, shining more light on it. It warmed Chester's back. "I ought to get going, my dear Karla. Everyone will be waking soon. Don't worry about us, because we'll be fine. I promise you that. I know it hurts you to hear that we're going to move on, but we must. Life has to go on. I'll come back and let you know how things turn out if I can. This is goodbye, but years down the road, I'll try to come back. I did knock down some of the markers, but I think I can find my way back without them if I had to."

Why was he being so wishy-washy? He had meant for this to be goodbye. No more returns. She would have to pay the price by never seeing him again. Why was it too much for him to bear? He couldn't think about his life without returning to her again. Karla had once been his whole life. But she wouldn't cooperate, despite how hard he worked to help her see the error of her ways. She just wouldn't listen.

Now it was time to move on and begin his new life with their daughter.

Chester rose and took his time getting back to the farmhouse. The sun beat down warming his back even as the frost crunched under his feet. By the time the farm was in sight, only frost in the shade remained.

He found Heather working in the barn with his parents.

"Heather, we need to talk. Come with me into the house."

She nodded and followed him without a word. Once inside he indicated for her to sit at the kitchen table. Chester sat next to her and didn't say anything for a minute.

She fidgeted without making eye contact.

Chester cleared his throat. "We're moving somewhere new. I can't tell you where, but it's quite a drive and we'll get a fresh start as a family. It's just what we need, don't you think?"

She stared at him, her skin looking pale.

"You're so excited you're speechless?" He smiled. "You'll love it and your new mom, too. She can't wait to meet you."

Other books by Stacy Claflin

Gone series

Gone

Held

Over

Complete Trilogy

Standalone

Dean's List (Lydia's story)

The Transformed Series

Deception (#1)

Betrayal (#2)

Forgotten (#3)

Silent Bite (#3.5)

Ascension (#4)

Duplicity (#5)

Sacrifice (#6)

Destroyed (#7)

Hidden Intentions (novel)

A Long Time Coming (Short Story)

Fallen (Novella)

Taken (Novella)

Seaside Hunters (Sweet Romance)

Seaside Surprises

Seaside Heartbeats

Seaside Dances

Seaside Kisses

Seaside Christmas

Other books

Chasing Mercy

Searching for Mercy

Visit StacyClaflin.com for details.

Sign up for new release updates.
http://stacyclaflin.com/newsletter/

Want to hang out and talk about books? Join My Book Hangout:
facebook.com/groups/stacyclaflinbooks/

and participate in the discussions. There are also exclusive giveaways, sneak peeks and more. Sometimes the members offer opinions on book covers too. You never know what you'll find.

Author's Note

Thanks so much for reading Gone. This is a story I've wanted to write for a long time but wanted to wait until I had more experience as a writer. It was a tough one to write. In fact, I had to take a couple months off because it was taking a toll on me emotionally. Once I came back, though, I was ready to get through the rest of it. I wrote the rest of the trilogy pretty quickly after that point. I hope you enjoy the trilogy and the characters as much as I do.

If you enjoyed this book, please consider leaving a review wherever you purchased it. Not only will your review help me to better understand what you like—so I can give you more of it!—but it will also help other readers find my work. Reviews can be short—just share your honest thoughts. That's it.

Want to know when I have a new release? Sign up here (stacy-claflin.com/newsletter) for new release updates. You'll even get a free ebook!

I've spent many hours writing, re-writing, and editing this work. I even put together a team who helped with the editing process. As it is impossible to find every single error, if you find any, please contact me through my website and let me know. Then I can fix them for future editions.

Thank you for your support!
~Stacy